CODENAME QUICKSILVER

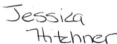

Sarah Dixon
Illustrated by Ann Johns

Designed by
Stephen Wright and David Gillingwater

Edited by Martin Oliver

Jessica Hitchner

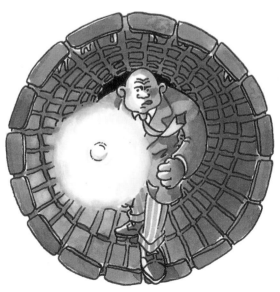

Map illustrations by David Gillingwater
Additional designs by Ann Johns

Series Editor: Gaby Waters

Contents

3   In Search of Quicksilver
4   Kidnap!
6   The Plot Thickens
8   Codename Quicksilver
10   Gang Gala Night
12   On the Trail of the Kidnappers
14   Eavesdropping
16   Secret Sequence
18   Stowaway!
20   Sewer Surprise
22   Subway Discovery
24   Going Underground
26   Peril in the Park
28   To the Surf Shack
30   Emergency Landing
32   Into Megabuck Towers
34   Crisis in the Control Room
36   Chaos
38   No Escape?
40   River Rendezvous
42   Clues
43   Answers

About this Book

Codename Quicksilver is a thrilling adventure story, packed with fiendish codes and puzzles which must be solved to unravel the plot. Most of the puzzles are pretty difficult, so don't be surprised if you get stuck. There are clues on page 42 and you will find all the answers at the back of the book. If you don't need to look at these, you may well be a genius.

In Search of Quicksilver

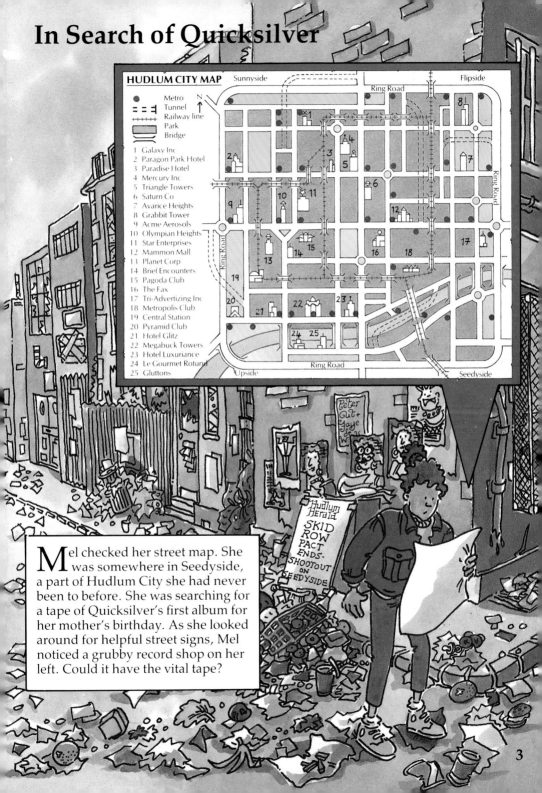

HUDLUM CITY MAP

Legend:
- Metro
- Tunnel
- Railway line
- Park
- Bridge

1 Galaxy Inc
2 Paragon Park Hotel
3 Paradise Hotel
4 Mercury Inc
5 Triangle Towers
6 Saturn Co
7 Avarice Heights
8 Grabbit Tower
9 Acme Aerosols
10 Olympian Heights
11 Star Enterprises
12 Mammon Mall
13 Planet Corp
14 Brief Encounters
15 Pagoda Club
16 The Fax
17 Tri-Advertizing Inc
18 Metropolis Club
19 Central Station
20 Pyramid Club
21 Hotel Glitz
22 Megabuck Towers
23 Hotel Luxuriance
24 Le Gourmet Rotund
25 Gluttons

Sunnyside · Flipside · Ring Road · Upside · Seedyside

Mel checked her street map. She was somewhere in Seedyside, a part of Hudlum City she had never been to before. She was searching for a tape of Quicksilver's first album for her mother's birthday. As she looked around for helpful street signs, Mel noticed a grubby record shop on her left. Could it have the vital tape?

3

Kidnap!

Those early Quicksilver tapes are all the rage.

QUICKSILVER MEMORABILIA

LIME-GREEN PLATFORM BOOTS from Great Crashing Festival '75 – Orlando, Marmalade Grove, Strawberry Fields – 432-556
GOLD-PLATED PLECTRUM AND DRUM KIT – drums in need of repair – Macavity, Surf Shack (pink hut with blue steps), Blondi Beach – no phone
FUZZBOX, GUITAR LEADS AND FESTIVAL PHOTOS – Thomas Katz esq, 10 Jerry Buildings, Rattingdean – 555533
ORANGE AND GREEN CATSUIT from Los Spangles Festival '73 – Felix, Rough Ride Ranch, Sierra Bravada – no phone

Mel waited while the assistant searched the shelves. At last he reappeared, shaking his head. The shop had sold out of Quicksilver tapes. What could she do now? The assistant sifted through a stack of dusty magazines and pulled out a grubby copy of "Deadbeat Express".

"Try skimming through the small ads," he suggested. "You might find the tape you want for sale there."

Mel wandered out of the shop and down the backstreets, scanning the pages. Everything a Quicksilver fan could want was for sale – except the tape. She stuffed the magazine in her pocket and looked around.

She was lost. Ahead she saw a man slouching against a wall. Perhaps he might help . . . or perhaps not, she decided, glancing up at his sinister face.

Mel hurried along the street. Suddenly she heard footsteps running towards her. There was a loud CRASH behind her. She glanced nervously over her shoulder, then . . . THUD!

Mel came to, her head spinning. As she tried to sit up, a man pressed something into her hand.

Suddenly a car screeched to a halt, inches away from Mel. Its doors flew open. The man looked around frantically, then ran . . .

But he was too late. Two men pounced on him. They dragged him to the car and bundled him inside. Then one of them turned and gave Mel a chilling stare. She recognized him instantly.

"One word of this and you're dead meat," he snarled.

The door slammed shut and the car roared away. Mel staggered to her feet, dazed and confused. She looked down the street. The car had vanished. There was no sign that anything had happened, except . . . Mel opened her hand and straightened out a crumpled sheet of paper with numbers and letters scrawled on it. It looked like some kind of code. Could it be a secret message?

What does it say?

The Plot Thickens

What did the message mean? Mel's mind was buzzing with questions when she noticed something strange. There, on the pavement, were yellow marks, like the footprints of someone running very fast – like the man who had been bundled into the car.

Mel glanced anxiously over her shoulder, then followed the footprints down a dark alley. The trail ended at an overturned pot of paint. There was a dead end ahead. Where had the man come from? Mel jumped as a door banged open above her and swung in the wind.

She crept nervously up the fire escape and stepped inside. In the gloom below was a vast, derelict factory.

Holding her breath, Mel began to tiptoe along the metal walkway. Suddenly a shout shattered the silence. Mel froze . . .

"Turn round slowly," a stern voice ordered.

Mel tried to keep calm and did as she was commanded. Dreading what she might see, she looked up hesitantly. She gulped hard. A shadowy figure was reaching for his inside pocket . . .

"Luke Jones, special agent, Investigations Inc," he growled, flashing a tattered ID card. "Who are you? Why are you here?"

The agent's number jumped into focus. In a flash Mel remembered the coded message. She slowly reached into her pocket and handed over the crumpled piece of paper.

The agent groaned. He stumbled past Mel into a room, collapsed in a shabby armchair and stared miserably at the coded writing.

"What's going on?" Mel asked.

Agent 153185 didn't reply. Instead he sprang to his feet and seized an old flying trophy.

To Mel's astonishment, the agent unscrewed the base and fished out a Quicksilver cassette. She gaped in disbelief as he slotted it into a tape deck . . . then winced. Quicksilver sounded even worse than she remembered. The agent scowled, flicked the STOP button and impatiently unravelled the tape.

"It's not what I expected," he muttered, looking puzzled. "And it's covered with scratches."

But there was something odd about the scratches . . . and the badly handwritten index card.

"Perhaps it's a code," Mel said. "If I work out what it says, will you explain what's going on?"

The agent looked at Mel, thought hard, then finally nodded, "Okay, it's a deal."

Can you decipher the code?

Codename Quicksilver

8

Gang Gala Night

Two hours later, Mel and Luke walked through the doors of the notorious Metropolis Club, haunt of hardened criminals and ruthless gangsters. The map message was their first lead. Now they knew that one of Aardvark's kidnappers would be in the club tonight.

"If you recognize anyone, give me a nod," Luke hissed. "Come on. Let's mingle."

Mel looked around doubtfully at the shady crowd.

"No, hang on, I've a better idea," Luke grinned. "We'll split up. I might recognize this Blade character from the I.I. crook files so I'll look for him and the instructions. Meet you by the exit at half past nine."

Feeling very out of place, Mel pushed her way to the bar. From there she could see everyone in the club – but what if she was recognized by the kidnapper? Mel shuddered and hastily grabbed a cocktail menu to hide her face.

It wasn't a cocktail menu. It was a seating plan for the Gang Gala Dinner. As she stared at the names, snatches of conversation drifted up from the dining tables below. In a flash, Mel realized she could identify Blade's seat. Now to grab the kidnapper's instructions . . .

Where is Blade's seat?

10

On the Trail of the Kidnappers

Al, I've got Chameleon's message. Jones has arrived with a meddling friend. I'll deal with the friend while you, Babs and Flash go ahead with the set-up as planned.

Mel took a deep breath, ready to slip over to Blade's seat for the instructions, but a man beat her to it. Mel froze as she glimpsed his familiar, sinister face.

The man carefully extracted a slip of paper from the folds of a napkin. Mel watched as he collared a surly waiter and hissed some instructions. The waiter nodded and the man walked towards the exit.

There was no time to lose. Mel raced after the kidnapper. As he hurried outside, a small scrap of paper fluttered out of his jacket. Mel hardly had time to glance at it before stuffing it in her pocket.

The man disappeared down an alley and into a multi-storey car park. Mel tracked him as far as the third level, then lost sight of him. She crept behind a taxi and scanned the rows of cars. Was that a figure unlocking a car door? She inched forward to get a closer look . . .

Suddenly she was blinded by headlights. Strong arms grabbed her. A piece of rag was shoved in her face. Everything went black.

Meanwhile, back in the club, Luke was still searching for Blade and the instructions. At half past nine he glanced over to the exit. Where was Mel? His gaze fell on to the waiter at the table ahead. Why was he looking so shifty? Luke's thoughts were cut short as he crashed into a fat stranger.

Before Luke could apologize, the fat man beamed at him, shook hands and disappeared. Luke turned his attention back to the waiter. He was scribbling something on a menu. He glanced up surreptitiously, as if to make sure the coast was clear, then slipped the menu under a red placemat.

As soon as the waiter disappeared behind the bar, Luke darted over to the table and grabbed the menu. He opened it and stared at . . . a list of dishes. But there were faint marks under some letters. Could it be yet another coded message?

Luke flipped through the cipher section of his I.I. Spy Fax to identify the code. There were three possibilities. But which was the right one?

What does the message say?

Eavesdropping

Mel opened her eyes and blinked. She was in a brightly-lit room. What had happened? Slowly she began to piece things together. The kidnap . . . the coded message . . . the Q tape . . . She dug in her pocket and pulled out a map, scraps of paper and a torn Deadbeat Express. The tape had gone. Her head still spinning, Mel staggered to the door and tugged at the handle.

The door was locked. But she could hear footsteps outside, heading her way. Someone was coming. What could they want? Mel didn't feel like finding out. She hid behind the door and waited . . . It swung open and in stomped the second kidnapper. Quick as a flash, Mel darted out behind him, slammed the door shut and rammed the bolts across.

Chameleon can't be with us tonight, but he left us this note sending his congratulations. Operation Quicksilver is going full steam ahead. Now we've got the tape and the photo, we don't need Aardvark.

We'll meet here at half past two tomorrow to divide the spoils.

Where was the tape?

We found it on a kid who saw the kidnap.

While the captive bellowed and hammered on the door, Mel sprinted up a flight of stairs into a long corridor. Suddenly a door opened behind her. Mel dived into a huge boardroom, wrenched open a cupboard and leapt inside. Her heart thudding, she peered out of a grill and watched a man march in. He scribbled a note, slapped it on the table and left.

Mel breathed a sigh of relief. She was just about to push the cupboard door open when the sinister kidnapper trooped into the room, followed by four shady strangers. Trapped in her cramped hiding place, Mel watched and listened hard. Who were these people? What was going on?

Who are they?

How shall we dispose of Aardvark?

I'll think about it. We've left him in the old ticket office at Grime Street Metro for the time being.

I've decoded the message on the tape. I'll show you the results in a minute. Now we need the photo.

Chameleon left me the combination so I'll get it out of the safe.

The kid's escaped! We've got to find her.

15

Secret Sequence

The room cleared instantly. Mel fell out of the cupboard, staggered to her feet and gulped. She was in the headquarters of the Syndicate, one of the three most ruthless gangs that stalked the city streets. And the Syndicate had the tape and the photo which would lead them to the secret Q formula. They had to be stopped, but how?

In a flash, Mel realized that the photo was still in the safe. If she found the photo, maybe she could beat the Syndicate to the formula.

Mel gave the dial on the safe an experimental twist. Immediately, a row of alarm lights began flashing. She snatched her hand away.

She had to find the combination fast. But where was it? As she looked around in desperation, Mel spotted the note that the sinister kidnapper had been holding. In their haste, the gang had left a vital clue.

What is the combination?

Piranha

page 1

Metunis of lsat mniteeg.

Fniwollog fruliae to tcark dwon Mtivacay, uuominans doisicen to cgnahe paln. Phnaria and Geppirr to garb Aravdrak and tpae. Cfia to ddocee Mytivaca's inoitcurtsns. Bbas and Fealh to rveirtee flumroa and pnalt Stacidnye ssirprue.

Tehn peecord wtih Ooitarepn Qevliskciur as pennald. Joe to bnirg beruhcors for our bugos ctirahy, the SPS (Steicoy for Poitcetorn of the Stacidnye) to nxet mniteeg. ivy to mkae cnuopmod Q.

I.I. pnidivorg olarevl stirucey for Mcubagek Trewos. Geppirr, Cnitroa and Al in pnoitisos V and W, and Coelemahn in red hetpociler on hapiled X (see paln of bnidliug) to dael wtih cesirs. Ecnegremy sangil - two tpas on red bepeelr bottun on wiklae-tiklae.

page 2

At 2.00 Joe to aserdds coitnevnon (in room mekrad Y - see paln of bnidliug) on blahef of SPS wlihe Ivy in cortnol room (Z) ppmus cnuopmod Q tguorhh air-cninoitidnog setsym. SPS (the Stacidnye) get ltos of sevlir - qciuk!

Fniwollog ilbativene ssecus of fnisiardnug, use cnuopmod Q to sziee cortnol of crtnuoy - tehn fllaniy the wlrod!

KING OF HEARTS

CIPHER OF THE DAY

CIPHER OF THE DAY

AYDW EV XUOH'I

Secu... uard
...er Hardman

Fyhqdxq-
Sedwhqjkbqjyedi
ed jxu weet meha.
Kdqrbu je ijqo veh
cuujydw. Fxeje
yd iqvu.
Secrydqjyed
kikab iyn-dkcruh
iugkudsu,jqhjyydw
myjx vylu.
Sxqcubued

CONVENTION OF THE CENTURY

The Fax - Friday 13th

STRETCH LIMOS will line Megabuck Avenue as the world's richest people flock to Megabuck Towers for tomorrow's spectacular charity convention.

Glamorous former film star and owner of Megabuck Towers, Fay de Way, told the **FAX** that the convention will be held in the glitzy VRP Club for Very Rich People, right at the top of the Towers.

MYSTERY MAN

Mystery millionaire, "Casino" Joe will kick off the proceedings at two o'clock with a speech on behalf of a new charity, the SPS. "This SPS is a lot of new-fangled nonsense!" silent screen sweetheart, Greta Garble told the **FAX**

BABS BALONEY, Chief Reporter

A vote at three o'clock will decide which lucky charity receives the millionaires' millions. Eccentric tennis ace, Ivor Lobb's Champions in Traction is the **FAX**'s hot favourite.

AMAZING DISCOVERY

"I hope everyone will give their money to my Donkeys in Distress"
Greta Garble

Megabuck Towers

An Introduction
– with pull-out plan
by
Karl Bunkl
RIBENA

$ ₣ £ ¥ $ ## SPS £ DM ¥ F $

Charity begins at home

Casino Joe, Chairman

Feeling hard-up? Lonely? Let the SPS take you by the hand and lead you to Norah and Gripper, fallen on hard times. The SPS cares about ordinary folk like Norah and Gripper. Dig deep into your pockets and give generously to the SPS. We'll make sure that all your donations go straight to Norah and Gripper and 11 other equally deserving cases.

Gripper, down on his luck

Norah, distressed gentry

Committee
L. Piranha, G.B. Hardman, B. Cortina, A. Terminator, B. Baloney, F. Capone, M. Metropolis, L. de Cifa, N. Kodar, A. Waits

Stowaway!

Six deft twists of the dial later, the safe door swung open. Mel reached right inside the safe until she found the photo. She shoved it in her pocket, then grabbed the playing card and the plan of Megabuck Towers from the table. She had a sneaking suspicion that they might prove useful.

Now Mel had to get out of the headquarters, fast. From every corner, alarm bells were clanging and sirens wailed.

Mel sprinted down the corridor, desperately looking for a way out. Suddenly she heard a yell. She had been spotted. There was a window ahead. Mel wrenched it open, took a deep breath and jumped . . .

Mel landed with a crunch in the yard below and dived into the back of an open van. She scrambled over a heap of cardboard boxes and hid behind a stack of crates.

More angry shouts rang out behind her. Mel froze as bright lights shone into the back of the van. But a long minute later, the lights snapped off and she was plunged back into darkness.

Mel sighed with relief. But she was not out of trouble yet. As she crawled out from her hiding place, the engine spluttered to life and the van lurched forwards.

The van rolled out of the HQ and turned right into the street. Mel could just make out a hoarse conversation. She shuddered as she caught the last, sinister words.

Hurry up, Gripper. You'll miss the rendezvous. We'll find that kid. No one ever escapes from the Syndicate alive.

Mel tried hard to memorize the van's route. As they accelerated, a train thundered overhead and in the distance she could hear the constant hum of the busy city.

The van shot through a red light, then screeched to a halt. A second set of traffic lights? While Gripper the driver revved the engine impatiently, Mel's mind clunked into gear. Now was her chance. She seized the door handle . . .

Suddenly the lights changed. Gripper stamped on the accelerator and veered sharply right. Mel went flying, along with boxes of frozen burgers, sauce bottles and buns.

Further on they swung right into a narrow street. Mel wiped a dollop of ketchup off her jacket and stared through the murky rear window at some shady characters lurking outside a warehouse.

Mel crossed her fingers, hoping they weren't going to stop in this seedy spot. She had seen enough gangsters for one day. Luckily Gripper seemed just as keen to keep going. With tyres squealing, he swerved left down a long, brightly-lit tunnel.

The van drove on through the seemingly endless tunnel. Mel gave up looking for landmarks and pulled out the photo she had taken from the safe. She held it up to the light and stared at the picture, and the writing below. For once it was a simple, uncoded message – or was it?

What is the message?

The Clique at large after graduation ceremony – Aardvark wearing his favourite wings from Red Baron Flying School – me before Vile Bodies gig – Bronsky recovering from unusually large quota of bean sprouts, mung beans, brown rice and chick peas.

Sewer Surprise

The van roared out of the tunnel and screeched to a halt in a dark backstreet. Gripper jumped out, levered up a manhole cover and disappeared down a deep shaft.

Mel decided to investigate. She climbed down after him into a long, dank, dripping tunnel. She could just make out his bulky shape in the murky gloom ahead. Further on, Gripper turned sharp left. Mel was plunged into pitch blackness. She blindly groped her way towards the turning, then . . .

SPLASH! Mel blundered into a foul-smelling stream of sludge. Gripper swivelled round.

"Come out!" he bellowed, beaming his torch along the dark tunnel. "It's no use hiding. I'll find you, wherever you are . . ."

Mel crouched in an old duct, hardly daring to breathe. Gripper walked slowly back down the passage towards her, playing his torch along the slimy walls. Any minute now, she would be discovered . . .

"Rats!" Gripper snorted.

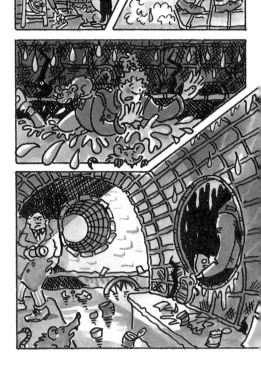

Gripper turned and trudged on. When the coast was clear, Mel crawled out of the duct. Soaking wet and dripping with slime, she squelched after him. Gripper stopped at a junction, wedged a small package into the brickwork, then scurried down the left fork.

Mel was about to reach for the package, when she saw a flicker of light at the end of the right-hand tunnel. A dark figure crept towards her . . . It was Luke. She waved at him eagerly.

"Mel?" Luke gasped, goggle-eyed in disbelief. "What happened? How did you get here?"

"What about you?" she asked. "Why are you here? For a moment I thought you were a gangster."

"I'm following a great new lead," Luke explained. "According to a message I found in the Metropolis Club, the Razor Gang have left a package at this very junction."

"That's strange!" Mel exclaimed. "I've been following a member of the Syndicate through the sewers – and this is what he left."

She pulled Gripper's package out of its niche and thrust it in Luke's hands. They peered at its contents in the torchlight.

"Now we know where Aardvark is," Luke beamed.

"I'm not so sure," Mel frowned.

Where does Luke think Aardvark is? What does Mel think?

Subway Discovery

They surfaced in Upside, slimy, bedraggled and confused. How could Aardvark be in two different places? The map appeared to be from the Razor Gang, but had been delivered by a Syndicate man. Luke decided it was a joint operation, but Mel was sceptical. From what she had seen at the Syndicate's HQ, this looked like a one-gang show.

"The only solution is to check out both locations," Luke said, after several minutes' deep thought. "Let's try Grime Street Metro first. That's the nearest."

The station was right on the other side of the city. Luke waved his I.I. ID card and tried to hail a taxi, but with no success.

At last, footsore and weary, they reached Grime Street. The entrance to the disused station was just visible between shuttered shops. Luke hastily scrambled through a gap in the boarding and looked around. He was in a dimly-lit hall.

CRASH! With a flying kick, Luke opened the ticket office door and leapt inside.

"FREEZE!" he yelled. "Hands up!"

But the room was deserted.

Then they heard muffled cries coming from a locker in the corner.

"Stand back!" cried Luke.

He wrenched the door open and a familiar figure slowly toppled out. They had found Dr Aardvark.

"Luke, I never thought you'd find me," gasped Aardvark as they cut him free. "And your friend . . . you're the girl I gave the message to!"

"The Syndicate will be here soon with more threats," he continued once Mel had introduced herself. "They're determined to find the Q formula, but as long as my tape is safe, they'll never succeed."

His happy smile turned into a look of horror when Mel explained what had happened to the tape.

"But why does the Syndicate want the Q formula?" Luke asked.

"They're hatching a sinister plot," Aardvark replied. "I don't know the details but I have my suspicions. Compound Q is a hypnotic gas. When used incorrectly, it becomes a brainwashing agent."

Mel shivered. Quickly, she told the others what she had found out about Operation Quicksilver.

What is the Syndicate's plan?

Going Underground

Suddenly there was a crash outside. The Syndicate had arrived. Luke smashed open the Emergency Exit.

"Head for the tunnel," he cried.

With the Syndicate hot on their heels, the trio stumbled down to the deserted platform. They leapt inside an abandoned train, raced through the carriages, then jumped out into a tunnel. Angry shouts echoed behind them as they sprinted along the track to the next station.

"Now change lines," Luke panted, charging down an escalator.

Closely pursued by the crooks, they ran on through station after station, leaving puzzled cleaners in their wake.

They had to change lines three times to shake off the Syndicate thugs. As Gripper's yells faded away down a distant tunnel, the exhausted trio hurried on to a sixth station. They staggered up a flight of stairs and collapsed at the top.

"We've got to beat the gang to the formula," Mel gasped. "I found Mac's photo in their HQ – but the message doesn't make sense, and neither does the one on the tape."

"Knowing Mac, the messages are in some kind of double cipher," said Aardvark. "Read them together."

Minutes later, the real message was revealed. Now they knew where the Q formula was hidden, but they had to find the fastest route there. As a train rumbled beneath them, Mel had a brainwave. They could take the metro. She fished out a metro map that she had picked up in Grime Street ticket office. But it was years out of date and all the names of the lines were missing.

Where do they need to go?
What is their most direct route?

Peril in the Park

Twenty minutes later, the breathless trio charged up the escalator of Paragon Place Metro and ran out into Paragon Park. Now to find the Quicksilver statue.

In the centre of the park stood the Retsinian Deities, ancient statues from the ransacked Temple of Ironika. Luke barged past two early morning strollers and gaped at the nameplates of the statues, puzzled. Which one was Quicksilver?

"Try the statue of Mercury," Aardvark grinned. "Quicksilver is another name for mercury."

With his penknife at the ready, Luke dashed towards Mercury. The statue's nameplate was loose, so he frantically started tugging it free from the plinth. Suddenly Mel noticed the glint of a metal wire behind the nameplate . . .

"STOP!" she yelled.

Just in time, all three dived for cover as a deafening explosion ripped through the park.

Luke reached out and clutched . . . a dismembered arm! For a second, he panicked, then he realized it was stone. He looked around, dazed.

"The Syndicate has beaten us to the formula," gasped Mel, staggering to her feet. "How can we stop Operation Quicksilver now?"

"There's only one person who can put a halt to the gang's sinister schemes," Aardvark groaned. "And that's Mac. Before he disappeared, he was developing a Q neutralizer."

"If only we knew where the thugs are holding him," Luke sighed.

"But they haven't got Mac," cried Mel, remembering a coded document she had seen at the Syndicate's HQ. "Either another gang took him . . . or maybe he wasn't kidnapped at all."

She looked at the photo that she had found in the safe. Mac's face looked very familiar. She was sure she had seen him only yesterday.

Minutes later, Aardvark hailed a taxi. Everyone bundled inside. Now to reach Mac, fast.

Where is he?

To the Surf Shack

Luke was first out of the taxi. He hurried across to the heliport and flashed his I.I. ID card at the crew in the control tower.

"I want a helicopter to Blondi Beach," he ordered. "Now."

"Wait a minute," the chief controller replied, eyeing Luke's card suspiciously. "You'll need special clearance, even if you are an I.I. agent."

"Clearance can wait," Aardvark hissed as the controller turned away. "Follow me."

He grabbed Luke and Mel, propelled them out of the building and bundled them into the nearest helicopter. They gaped at the scientist, dumbstruck.

"I was the star pupil at the Red Baron School of Flying," Aardvark grinned as he seized the joystick.

Two hours later, the helicopter was hovering over Blondi Beach. Mel scanned the beach below for Mac's hideaway, the Surf Shack.

Minutes later, Aardvark landed outside a weather-beaten shack with peeling pink paint and grubby windows. Mel ran up the steps and hammered on its battered door.

There was no reply. Mel tried again . . . and again.

"Looks like no one's at home," Luke muttered, peering through a cracked, salt-sprayed windowpane.

They looked at each other glumly. They had flown all this way to find Mac and he wasn't even in.

Mel wandered over the dunes to the shore and watched surfers ride the huge rollers. A lone surfer sauntered back towards the shack. She stared at him . . .

"Professor Macavity?" she called. But the surfer kept on walking.

"The Syndicate's found the Q formula," Mel continued.

"Who are you?" hissed Mac, stopping dead in his tracks. "What do you know about the Q formula?"

Mac listened to Mel's story, but when he saw Luke sitting on the steps of the shack, he bristled.

"What are you doing with HIM?" he demanded. "Everyone knows about him and his gangster friends. It's all over today's newspaper."

It couldn't be true! For a second Mel gaped in disbelief at the paper lying by the step. Then everything fell into place. Luke had been framed – and she could prove it.

How?

The Fax

I.I. SCANDAL – AGENT LINK WITH GANG BOSS

BABS BALONEY, Chief Reporter

THE FAX can reveal that the youngest member of the world-famous secret agency, Investigations Inc, is working for the ruthless godfathers of the city's seedy underworld.

The FAX caught Jones red-handed, consorting with notorious gangland boss Jake the Toad at the Metropolis Club last night.

"We're best buddies, especially after the Prima Tua deal," laughed the Toad when the FAX rang him at his luxury penthouse flat. "He's also a close pal of Syndicate top gun, Baby Cortina."

HUDLUM JAILBREAK

Cortina is on the run, following his escape from Hudlum Island high security jail. Prison sources say that someone in the secret agencies must have been in the know. Was this someone Luke Jones? The FAX demands the FACTS.

Emergency Landing

Mac disappeared into his shack and emerged five seconds later, brandishing a canister of Q neutralizer. Everyone piled into the helicopter and soon Blondi Beach was a blurr on the horizon.

Two hours later, they were flying over the city. Mel glanced at her watch. In half an hour, Operation Quicksilver would begin.

"We're running out of fuel fast," Aardvark gulped. "We'll have to land soon."

A red warning light flashed on the control panel as they hovered over Megabuck Towers.

"Where can I land?" Aardvark cried, gripping onto the joystick.

Suddenly the fuel gauge clicked to zero. The engine began to splutter ominously . . .

"WHERE?" screamed Aardvark.

Mel's brain sprang into action. She pulled out the Syndicate's plan of the skyscraper. They had to get to the control room, but only one landing pad led there. Could she find it in time?

Where can they land?

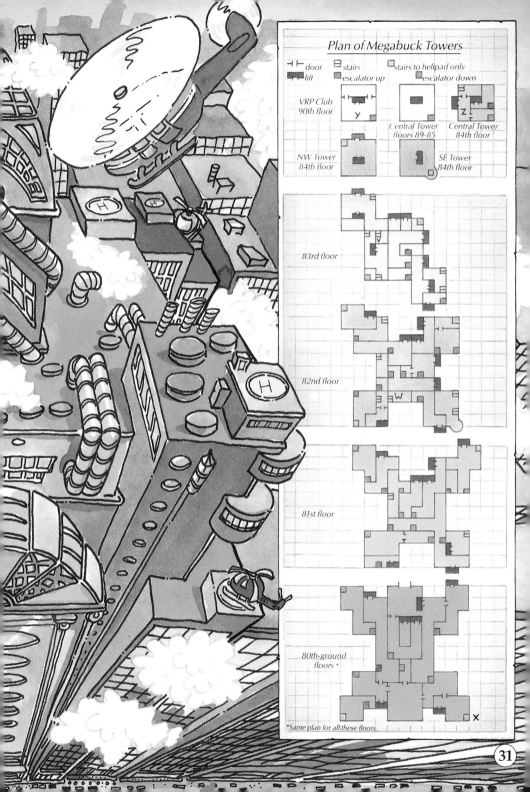

Into Megabuck Towers

Mel gaped out of the cockpit in horror as the helicopter spiralled downwards. At the last minute, Dr Aardvark wrenched the joystick up. The helicopter hovered in mid-air, then crash-landed on the south-east tower. Aardvark pulled the others out of the juddering wreck. They looked around, dazed.

"Th-th-that was a close shave," Luke stammered.

"Look out!" Aardvark yelled.

With a great CRACK, a rotor blade shot off the helicopter and whistled past Luke's left ear, missing it by inches.

Mel staggered to her feet and was nearly blown off the edge of the tower by a sudden gust of wind.

"Get to the door!" Mac ordered, grabbing hold of her. "Three narrow escapes are enough for one day."

With a roar, the wind smashed against the helicopter, ripping away the remaining rotors and shattering the windows. Lethal fragments cut through the air as the four dashed across the roof. Up ahead, Luke tried to radio through to the I.I. agents providing security for the convention, but all he could get was static.

At last they reached the door – but it was locked. How could they get in? Luke stared blankly at the keys on the entry panel. Then he remembered. Quickly, he punched in his agent and organization numbers in I.I. code. The door clicked open and everyone dived inside Megabuck Towers.

Clutching the plan tightly, Mel led the way to the control room. They whizzed between floors in lifts, charged down escalators, puffed and panted up stairs, and finally piled into a service lift.

The lift stopped with a jolt right outside the control room. But its doors remained firmly shut. A message flickered across a small screen in front of them, "Enter Access Number".

Luke keyed in his agent number. Nothing happened. He tried putting his number into every code he knew, but it was hopeless.

"Is there a special security sequence for the day?" Mel asked. "Would I.I. HQ have it?"

Luke anxiously radioed through. The four listened to HQ's reply with bated breath . . .

Mel's heart sank. Any minute now, Operation Quicksilver would begin . . . and succeed, all because they were trapped in a lift.

They would never work out the secret sequence to open the lift door. The information from HQ was useless – or was it?

What is the sequence?

Control Room Crisis

Everyone held their breath as Mac tapped in the secret sequence. Only the lift door separated them from a ruthless Syndicate villain.

Suddenly the lift door slid open. They stared into the control room. Mac and Aardvark gasped . . .

Dr Bronsky! Their missing colleague was crouching over a large air-conditioning vent, armed with a gleaming metallic cylinder of Q gas. So she had been a member of the sinister gang all the time.

"STOP!" Mac bellowed.

Dr Bronsky spun round and released a jet of Q gas straight at him. Mac ducked just in time. Quickly, Mel grabbed the canister of Q neutralizer from Mac and pressed the trigger. There was a long HISS of escaping gas.

"Compound Q is harmless now," Mel grinned. "I've neutralized it. Operation Quicksilver has failed."

Luke, Mac and Aardvark leapt out of the lift and tied Bronsky up. The evil scientist sneered at them.

"You may have caught me, but you're too late!" she smirked. "I've already contaminated the air-conditioning system with Q."

"Hurry!" Mac cried. "Pump the neutralizer up the vent."

"You'll need to switch on the system first," Bronsky laughed.

"Where's the ON button?" squawked Luke, pointing at hundreds of controls.

Bronsky watched with glee as the four jabbed buttons, twisted dials and pulled levers, throwing every system into overdrive – except the air-conditioning system.

Where WAS the button? Mel looked around desperately. Out of the corner of her eye, through a haze of steam and flashing lights, she saw Bronsky's foot tap twice against a small walkie-talkie.

"That's the Syndicate distress signal," Bronsky purred. "My friends are coming to get you. There's no escape."

As if on cue, the lift began to open and footsteps thundered down a nearby passage. Mel kept cool. She knew Bronsky was wrong. There was an escape route – and a few vital seconds left to find the ON button.

Where is the escape route?

Chaos

Just before Bronsky's sidekicks burst in, Luke punched a small red button. With a great whoosh, the neutralizer was sucked through the system. As the four ran out of the room, Mac grabbed Bronsky's case.

"Take this to I.I. HQ," he hissed to Luke. "The Q formula's inside."

They raced down to the 82nd floor, took a wrong turning up an escalator and jumped into a huge gilt lift. It zoomed upwards.

To their surprise, they stepped out of the lift into the VRP Club. Mel blinked, dazzled by sparkling chandeliers. A fat, cigar-wielding man was addressing the convention. He was Casino Joe of the Syndicate and he was just finishing his phony spiel.

" . . . and that's why you must give all your money to the SPS," he smiled. "Hands up if you agree."

Had the neutralizer reached the club in time? Mel watched Casino Joe's audience anxiously . . .

"Hold on," yelled a woman. "What about Donkeys in Distress?"

At once, everyone began shouting. Casino Joe's smile turned into a snarl. He glanced at the lift and caught Mel's look of triumph.

Just then the lift doors opened behind Mel. Gripper, Al and Cortina leapt out, disguised as security guards. The VRPs dived for cover, scattering files and papers, as Luke vaulted across the conference table and raced for the escalator, clutching the case. Casino Joe and his cronies charged after him.

"We'll take care of this one!" Joe cried to a huddle of I.I. agents in the corner. "You get the rest!"

The agents promptly pounced on Mel, Mac and Aardvark.

"You're making a BIG mistake," Mel shouted, struggling to break free from the agents. "The real villains are getting away."

As Gripper swung past on a chandelier and disappeared after Luke, Mel tried to explain about Operation Quicksilver and the Syndicate to the sceptical agents.

"You MUST believe me," she insisted. "We've left one of them tied up in the control room."

"You'd better be right," an agent muttered, then took out his radio. "Put all staff on red alert . . ."

Mel's watch bleeped 2.30. In a flash she realized that they could round up the rest of the gang at their secret meeting . . . if only she could remember where their HQ was.

Where is the Syndicate's HQ?

No Escape?

With Casino Joe, Cortina, Gripper and Al hard on his heels, Luke zigzagged through the upper floors of Megabuck Towers, desperately clinging on to Mac's case.

By the 81st floor, the Syndicate crooks were still on his trail. If only he could shake them off. Quickly, Luke leapt into the first lift he saw and jabbed the down button. With alarming speed, the lift plunged hundreds of feet into the glass foyer below. Luke waited for his stomach to catch up with him, then dashed to the entrance.

"There's no escape," a voice growled. "Hand over the case."

The four Syndicate heavies barred his escape. Luke gritted his teeth and swung the case through the glass wall.

He clambered through the jagged hole onto the pavement and dodged past bewildered tourists.

"You haven't seen the last of us yet!" Gripper bellowed behind him.

Cars squealed to a halt, horns blaring angrily, as Luke darted across the road to the river. On the opposite bank, he could just make out the I.I.'s HQ – and safety.

Gasping for breath, Luke raced along the endless embankment. At last he reached a bridge. Close to exhaustion, he stumbled across.

Suddenly a car swerved in front of him. Cortina and Casino Joe jumped out. Al and Gripper were catching him up. He was trapped, unless . . .

Blood pounding in his ears, Luke hoisted himself on to the girders of the bridge and began to climb. The case grew heavier and heavier . . .

At the top Luke clung to a metal support. He could go no further. A helicopter whirred above him. Help at last. A rope ladder dropped from the hatch and a man with a megaphone leaned out. Luke smiled, relieved, as he recognized the friendly face of the I.I. captain.

"You can hand the case to me now!" the captain shouted.

As Luke held out the case, a car zoomed on to the bridge, sending the crowds surging back, and screeched to a halt. Suddenly he heard a high-pitched voice above the commotion . . .

"Don't do it!" Mel yelled.

Why not?

River Rendezvous

With a snarl, the captain lunged for the case. But Luke was not going to let him or the Syndicate heavies have it. Taking a deep breath, he dived into the depths of the murky river below.

Luke surfaced spluttering, but still clutching the vital case. A speedboat carefully drew up beside him and Aardvark threw him a rope.

Dripping and bewildered, Luke clambered aboard. Over his shoulder, he watched as detectives dragged the furious I.I. captain from his helicopter.

"What's going on?" he asked.

"The Syndicate's been smashed," Mel explained. "All 13 members have been captured, including the gang's ruthless leader, Chameleon, alias the I.I.'s double-crossing captain."

"Operation Quicksilver has been a total failure," laughed Aardvark.

"Have you got my case?" Mac asked. "Is the Q formula safe?"

Luke proudly handed over the case. Then, with a sinking feeling, he noticed that the clasps were broken. Mac gaped inside, horrorstruck.

"It must have fallen out," Luke mumbled. "Why is it so important? We've got the neutralizer."

"We don't want the Q formula to fall into the wrong hands again," gulped Mac. "We might not be able to foil another sinister plot in time."

"Don't panic," Aardvark grinned. "I know where the formula is."

Where is it?

Friday 27th

DIVING DISCOVERY

Former secret agent and new Olympic hopeful, Luke Jones, sponsored by the FAX. Pics of Jones's dramatic diving debut in full on p.3.

SINISTER SYNDICATE PLOT FOILED

ROSY PARKER,
Chief Reporter

THE SYNDICATE, one of the three ruthless gangs that rule the city's seedy underworld has been BUSTED. Their fiendish plot to seize control of the world has been foiled, thanks to plucky Mel Lee and junior secret agent Luke Jones.

In the first stage of the gang's sinister plan, Syndicate member and gambling king Casino Joe posed as a bogus charity boss and tried to con millions from multi-millionaires at the VRP charity convention.

But Mel and Luke scotched Casino's crooked scheme. In a dramatic chase, Casino our cronies were rounded Rusty Gate Suspension Bridge.

rest of the Syndicate picked up at a secret eeting in the gang's penthouse HQ off Avarice Avenue.

HI MOM

SYNDICATE SHOCK

Last night, in an exclusive FAX interview, Mel Lee revealed that the Syndicate's mystery boss and criminal mastermind, Chameleon was none other than I.I. CAPTAIN JOHN SILVER.

"I can't believe it," stunned silver-haired I.I. receptionist, Beryl Twinset told the FAX. "He was such a nice man."

Syndicate members include a leading banker, an accountant, a top spy, a reporter and a missing scientist working on a top-secret project codenamed Quicksilver.

RIVAL GANGS' GLEE

AS ALL 13 MEMBERS of the Syndicate cooled their heels in Hudlum Island High Security Jail last night, rival gangsters from the Jemmies and Razor Gang celebrated at Blade's Bar (formerly the Metropolis Club).

"We're delighted at the news," a relieved Ronnie Razor told the FAX. "The Syndicate broke the Skid Row Pact, then tried to frame us and the emmies for everything they did. Good riddance!"

COVER-UP?

One question remains. HOW did the Syndicate intend to achieve their final aim of world domination? Is there a COVER-UP? The FAX demands the FACTS.

Sunday 15th

AMAZING VRP CHARITY DECISION

AFTER a dramatic beginning, the glitzy VRP Charity Convention reached an astonishing climax. Glamorous former film star and owner of Megabuck Towers, Fay de Way announced that the multi-millionaires voted to give their millions to ALL the charities.

"Every charity will benefit," explained Donkeys in Distress president Greta Garble. "Except that bogus Syndicate outfit, the SPS!"

Last night Fay de Way told the FAX she is turning Megabuck Towers into a fabulous THEME PARK.

PARTY TIME

The building will be full of AMAZING MAZES and FUN RIDES – and it will all be FREE. Before the builders move in, there will be a huge party. EVERYONE in the city is invited.

Surf Shack
Blondi Beach

Jammer
X

Dear Mel,
Here's that Quicksilver tape you were looking for.
Happy listenin
drum kit?
en plectru
mer Aard
Shack?
ng Qui
Love
Mac

12c Arcadian Ave
Sunnybrook
Spring County

Dear Mac,
Thanks for the tape. Mum's over the moon and plays it all the time. I've just bought myself some earplugs!
Can't wait to see you, Dr Aardvark and the Olympic hopeful at Blondi Beach next summer.
Love Mel X

41

Clues

Pages 4-5

Try substituting letters for numbers and numbers for letters.

Pages 6-7

Line up the scratches with the letters below and try reading downwards. Remember the previous message. Don't worry if your solution doesn't make sense.

Pages 8-9

Try rearranging the letters between the first and last letter of each word. Can you match the symbols with those on the map on page 3?

Pages 10-11

Solve this by a process of elimination. Which tables can you rule out? You don't need to work out where everyone sits.

Pages 12-13

Read the letters above the dots, then try applying the codes in Luke's Spy Fax.

Pages 14-15

Has the sinister kidnapper mentioned any of his associates? Look at the woman with grey hair.

Pages 16-17

Look at the playing card for the cipher. How can KING OF HEARTS become AYDW EV XUQHJI?

Pages 18-19

Have you spotted the dots? Don't worry if your solution doesn't make sense.

Pages 20-21

Do you recognize this code? Is the map the right way round? And what did Mel overhear at the secret meeting?

Pages 22-23

Read the coded minutes on page 16. They are in a familiar code.

Pages 24-25

This is tricky. Reverse the order of the words in each message and try combining them to make a sentence. You may have to crack the code by trial and error. Before you can work out where the trio must go, you have to find out where they are. Look at the names of the lines and the order in which they appear. Remember they have changed lines three times and have reached their sixth station.

Pages 26-27

Look back. Remember Mac's full name.

Pages 28-29

Try decoding the message dropped by the sinister kidnapper on page 12. Use the playing card cipher.

Pages 30-31

Look at the coded minutes on page 16. This is a three-dimensional maze.

Pages 32-33

This is easy.

Pages 34-35

Where are the gangsters positioned?

Pages 36-37

Look back to Mel's journey on pages 18 and 19. Can you match up the route with the map on page 3? Can you find the name of the street? Try comparing the map on page 3 with the metro map on page 25.

Pages 38-39

Do you recognize the helicopter? Have you seen this man before?

Page 40

Look back and use your eyes.

Answers

Pages 4-5

The numbers represent letters and the letters represent words, so that 1=A and A=1, 2=B and B=2, and so on to the end of the alphabet. With punctuation and spaces added, the decoded message says:

AGENT 15 3 18 5 – THEY ARE ON TO ME. THE Q TAPE IS IN THE RED BARON. MAKE SURE THEY NEVER FIND IT. THE FIRST WORD IS PARK. – AARDVARK

Pages 6-7

Mel uses the scratches on the tape to decipher the code. First she positions the tape above the first line, placing the first scratch above the letter P. Then she reads down the column of letters below the scratch. This produces the word PARK. Mel reveals the rest of the message by reading down the columns below the other scratches. The complete message is:

PARK IN STATUE NAMEPLATE HIDDEN IS

This may not make sense but Mel is sure she has decoded the message correctly because the coded message on page 5 told her "the first word is park".

Pages 8-9

The letters between the first and last letters of each word on the intercepted message are written in reverse order. The first and last letters remain the same. Decoded, the message says:

CHAMELEON – GRIPPER AND I PICKED UP AARDVARK BUT WE COULD NOT FIND THE Q TAPE. SEND FURTHER INSTRUCTIONS TO BUILDING MARKED X ON MAP. LEAVE THEM UNDER NAPKIN AT BLADE'S SEAT. I WILL COLLECT THEM AT NINE – PIRANHA

The symbols below the message match some of those on the city map. This suggests that they are a map of some sort. If you superimpose them on Mel's map of Hudlum City, you can see that X marks the position of building 18, the Metropolis Club.

The matching symbols are marked in green.

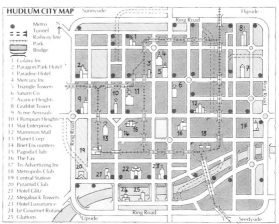

Pages 10-11

Mel can locate Blade's seat by a process of elimination. She correctly assumes that the people at the dining tables are sitting in their places and she knows that Blade has not arrived yet, because the woman in green at table A says so. It is also clear from what she is saying that Blade will sit at another table, so Mel can rule out the empty seat at table A.

According to the thin waiter speaking to Mr Metropolis, no members of rival gangs are sitting at the same table.

With the aid of the seating plan and snippets of conversation, Mel can identify the man at table B as Goldfingers Loot of the Jemmies and the woman at table D as Babs Baloney of the Syndicate. As Blade is a member of the Razor Gang, he cannot sit at either table.

Mel can also identify the man at the table in the bar area to her left as Officer Carver of the Razor Gang. He will be sitting right behind Krystal the singer. The only seats left that allow him to do this are at tables B and E. He will be sitting at E.

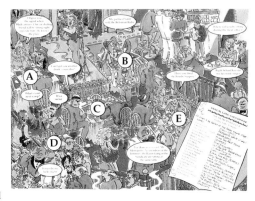

But Blade cannot sit in the seat opposite Officer Carver on table E, as the woman in green at table A says he will be sitting right opposite a car dealer.

This leaves table C. As Blade cannot be sitting opposite the man addressed as councillor, he is left with the seat opposite the man in the white hat, who must be the car dealer.

Pages 12-13

To decipher the message, Luke first reads the letters above the dots then divides them into blocks of four, as instructed by his I.I. Spy Fax. This is the result:

TKAE PCAK AEGT OUJN CITO NINN ENIS EEWR STAT WAOM ADNL EVAE IUNS ULAP LCAE

By a process of elimination, Luke works out that the message is in Razor Muddle Code. When he follows the instructions in his Spy Fax, this message is revealed:

TAKE PACKAGE TO JUNCTION NINE IN SEWERS AT TWO AM AND LEAVE IN USUAL PLACE.

Pages 14-15

According to Luke, Aardvark's kidnap is the work of either the Syndicate, the Jemmies or the Razor Gang. As the gangs have fallen out and broken the Skid Row Pact after a shootout on Seedyside (pages 3 and 9), it is unlikely that more than one gang is involved in the kidnap.

In the intercepted message on page 9, one of the kidnappers arranges to pick up further instructions under a napkin at Blade's seat in the Metropolis Club. Mel knows from the seating plan on page 11 that Blade is a member of the Razor Gang. This suggests that Blade might be involved and that the kidnap is the work of the Razor Gang.

But after Piranha, the sinister kidnapper, picks up the instructions, Mel overhears him tell the large waiter on page 12 "You, Babs and Flash go ahead with the set-up as planned". He is obviously referring to Babs Baloney and Flash Capone who are listed on the seating plan as members of the Syndicate. This seems to suggest that Aardvark's kidnap was a Syndicate operation. Mel finds this very confusing.

At the secret meeting, Mel rules out the Razor Gang in face of strong evidence pointing to the Syndicate. She decides Blade was not involved in the kidnap and his seat was just used as a message drop.

Pages 14-15 (continued)

When the grey-haired woman enters the room, she makes a secret signal which Mel recognizes instantly. It is the secret Syndicate gang salute, which Mel saw on television (page 8) during a news report on Baby Cortina, the escaped Syndicate gangster. If you flip back to the Metropolis Club, you can see other members of the gang using this secret signal.

Pages 16-17

Mel spots the playing card with CIPHER OF THE DAY written on it. She notices that the strange words AYDW EV XUQHJI on the bottom of the card have the same number of letters in the same grouping as the words KING OF HEARTS on the top of the card. Mel realizes that AYDW EV XUQHJI is KING OF HEARTS written in a shifted alphabet code which starts with K and ends with J so that K=A, L=B, M=C and so on. The note on yellow paper is written in the same alphabet. Decoded, it says:

PIRANHA, CONGRATULATIONS ON THE GOOD WORK. UNABLE TO STAY FOR MEETING. PHOTO IN SAFE. COMBINATION – USUAL SIX-NUMBER SEQUENCE STARTING WITH FIVE. CHAMELEON

Assuming that a sequence is a regular pattern of numbers, there is only one possible six-number sequence on the dial. It is 5 7 11 17 25 35. The jump between the numbers increases by two each time.

Pages 18-19

Mel spots faint dots below some of the letters which reveal this incomprehensible message:

QALUMROFDNIHEBFOREVLISKCIUQNO GARAP

When this message is read backwards and spaces are added, it forms these words:

PARAGON QUICKSILVER OF BEHIND FORMULA Q

They do not make sense, but neither did Mac's previous message on the Q tape.

Pages 20-21

Like the message on page 13, this message is in Razor Muddle Code. Decoded, it says:

JACK, JOIN RING ROAD AT ACME AEROSOLS AND HEAD SOUTH. TAKE FIRST RIGHT TURNING OFF RING ROAD. TURN ONTO NORTHWEST BOUND ROAD AT FIRST JUNCTION. AT NEXT JUNCTION TAKE ROAD HEADING DUE NORTH. STOP AT FIRST TOWN. DROP AARDVARK OFF AT CARVER MOTEL. BLADE

The blue road on this map is the ring road. When Luke compares the postions of the turnings off the ring road with those on Mel's map on page 3, he realizes that this map is the wrong way round and that north is pointing to the bottom left-hand corner. Now it is easy to follow the directions. The route is marked in black and it leads to Fumesburg.

Mel cannot believe that Aardvark is at Fumesburg. At the secret meeting on page 14 she overheard Piranha, the sinister kidnapper, say that Aardvark was in the old ticket office at Grime Street Metro. She is very confused. From what she has seen, this is a Syndicate operation. But she cannot understand why the Syndicate man, Gripper, left a Razor Gang message. She wonders whether this might be a false trail laid by the Syndicate to make Luke think it is the work of the Razor Gang.

While Mel was searching for the safe's combination on page 16, she read the newspaper cutting about the Charity Convention and the coded minutes. This is what the minutes say:

Minutes of last meeting

Following failure to track down **Macavity**, unanimous decision to change plan. **Piranha** and **Gripper** to grab **Aardvark** and tape. **Cifa** to decode **Macavity's** instructions. **Babs** and **Flash** to retrieve formula and plant Syndicate surprise.

Then proceed with Operation Quicksilver as planned. Joe to bring brochures for our bogus charity, the SPS (Society for Protection of the Syndicate) to next meeting. **Ivy** to make compound Q.

I.I. providing overall security for Megabuck Towers. **Gripper**, **Cortina** and **Al** in positions V and W, and **Chameleon** in red helicopter on helipad X (see plan of building) to deal with crises. Emergency signal – two taps on red bleeper button on walkie-talkie.

At 2.00 **Joe** to address convention (in room marked Y – see plan of building) on behalf of the SPS while **Ivy** in control room (Z) pumps compound Q through air-conditioning system. SPS (the Syndicate) get lots of silver – quick!

Following inevitable success of fundraising, use compound Q to seize control of country – then finally the world!

Now that Aardvark has explained that compound Q is a hypnotic gas which can be used as a brainwashing agent, Mel instantly realizes what the gang's fiendish plan is. They intend to use compound Q to brainwash the millionaires at the Megabuck Towers Charity Convention into handing all their money to the SPS, a bogus charity run by the Syndicate for their own benefit. Then the evil gang will use compound Q to take over the country, and then the world.

First of all, they have to find the hiding place of the Q formula. To crack Mac's double cipher, they must put the two messages together. This is tricky as there is no obvious way of combining the messages. After a process of trial and error, they reverse the order of the words in each part of the message. The first message now says:

IS HIDDEN NAMEPLATE STATUE IN PARK

The second message now says:

Q FORMULA BEHIND OF QUICKSILVER PARAGON

Then they take two words from the second message, then two from the first, then one from the second and one from the first, then two words from each message again, then one from each. This reveals the final message:

Q FORMULA IS HIDDEN BEHIND NAMEPLATE OF QUICKSILVER STATUE IN PARAGON PARK.

To find the most direct route to Paragon Park, they must first work out where they are. Since they left Grime Street, they have changed lines three times to reach the sixth station. When they remember the names of the lines in some of the stations they have run through, they realize there is only one route that they could have taken. It leads to Hotel Glitz.

After matching up the placenames and positions of the metro stations on the metro map with Mel's map of Hudlum City, they can see that Paragon Place is the nearest station to Paragon Park.

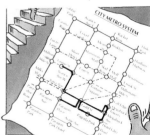

Their route from Grime Street to Paragon Park via Hotel Glitz is marked in black.

Pages 26-27

Mel has seen Mac's face before, on a television screen on page 8. The location, Blondi Beach, reminds her of an advert in the Quicksilver Memorabilia section of Deadbeat Express (page 4) – Macavity, Surf Shack, Blondi Beach. Mel knows that Mac's full name is Professor Macavity and remembers Luke telling her that Mac was a Quicksilver fan, so she realizes that this must be Mac's address.

Theresa Green, Blondi Beach

Pages 28-29

In her pocket, Mel has a message on pink paper, dropped by Piranha, the sinister kidnapper, on page 12. Now she has the playing card with the cipher of the day, she realizes the message on the pink paper is in the same code as the note on yellow paper (page 17). Decoded, the message provides her with proof that Luke has been framed. This is what it says:

PIRANHA – I SUSPECT AGENT 153185 KNOWS WHERE THE TAPE IS. HE WILL BE HERE TONIGHT. YOU AND AL TO SET TRAP. DISAPPEARANCE TO BE EXPLAINED BY BABS' AND FLASH'S I.I. SCANDAL FRAME-UP STORY IN TOMORROW'S FAX – CHAMELEON

Pages 30-31

From the coded minutes on page 16, Mel knows they will find a member of the Syndicate called Ivy with compound Q in the control room marked Z. To get there, they should land on the helipad on the south-east tower and follow the route marked in black.

They should land here.

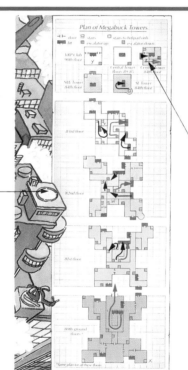

Door on east wall.

Pages 32-33

This sequence proved to be surprisingly simple. It is 4 6 5 7 6 8 7 9. The jumps between the numbers increase by two, then decrease by one, then increase by two again and increase by one, and so on.

Pages 34-35

Their escape route from the control room is through the door on the east wall. This route avoids the Syndicate gangsters who have run from positions V and W in response to Bronsky's emergency signal and are about to enter the control room via the lift and the door on the north wall.

Their escape route is marked in red on the plan above.

Pages 36-37

The Syndicate's secret HQ is at 13 Avarice Avenue.

Mel works this out by remembering the route taken by Gripper's van from the HQ on pages 18 and 19. She matches up this route and the landmarks she saw through the van's rear window with her map of the city. The route is marked in red.

To find out the name of the street where the Syndicate's HQ is located, Mel compares the positions of the metro stations on her map of the city with those on the metro map (page 25). From this she realizes that the HQ is on Avarice Avenue. Fortunately she was able to spot the number – 13, unlucky for some!

Here is the view looking west from this junction

Railway bridge
First right turn
Second right turn
Left turn down the tunnel

Avarice Ave W Metro   Avarice Ave E Metro

Pages 38-39

The I.I. captain is none other than Chameleon, the shadowy leader of the Syndicate. Thinking back to the coded minutes and the plan of Megabuck Towers, Mel knows that Chameleon is in the red helicopter in the position marked X. When they are hovering over the skyscraper on page 31, she can see Chameleon's helicopter below. The I.I. captain is flying an identical red helicopter. Even its number is the same.

More important still, Mel has seen the I.I. captain before – in the Syndicate HQ on page 15. She watched him write a note which she later decoded to find the safe combination. The note was signed "Chameleon".

Geniuses and serious decoders might have had their suspicions about the I.I. captain before now. If Luke's agent and organization numbers are encoded to make the words OCAHE LEON on page 32, what word do the I.I. captain's agent and organization numbers form using the same code?

Page 40

The vital Q formula fell out of the case in the lift that Luke jumped into on the 81st floor (page 38). Luckily the Syndicate thugs were in the other lift, so they did not pick it up. Fortunately Aardvark spotted it lying on the floor when he, Mel and Mac were finding their way out of Megabuck Towers.

COBRA CONSIGNMENT

Sarah Dixon

Illustrated by Ann Johns

Contents

51 Off to Magnos
52 Distress at Sea
54 Ransacked!
56 Familiar Faces
58 To the Ancient City
60 A Bizarre Meeting
62 Magazine Message
64 Clifftop Chase
66 Vital Information
68 The Plot Thickens
70 A Secret Cipher
72 The Final Consignment

74 Into the Base
76 Prisoners in the Labyrinth
78 In Search of the COBRA
80 Sabotage
82 The Palace of Doom
84 Farewell Cobradiki
86 The COBRA Project
88 Cobra Gold
90 Clues
91 Answers

About this Book

Cobra Consignment is a thrilling adventure story, packed with fiendish puzzles which must be solved to unravel the plot. If you get stuck – and you may – there are clues on page 42 to point you in the right direction. You will find all the answers at the back of the book. If you don't need to look at these, you may be a genius.

Off to Magnos

As the hot, airless bus hurtled along the road to the port, Nat pulled out a crumpled letter. It had only arrived a week ago and he had read it countless times since then. Cousin Al, the famous archeologist, had invited him to the island of Magnos to help on his latest dig. It sounded too good to be true – two weeks of sun, sea and ancient treasure! There had to be a catch somewhere …

Villa Magnotaur
Magnotaur Passage
Town Wall
Magnos Town

Dear Nat,
How do you like the sound of two weeks on the sunny island of Magnos? The ex-film star, Strega Nimbus (remember Battlestar Elektra?) has organized a new excavation of the ancient city above Magnos Town. She's convinced that its ruins hold the key to the whereabouts of the legendary treasure of Magnos, the so-called Cobra Gold. I'm in charge of the dig and I desperately need more help. So far there's only me, my assistant, Lina, and, occasionally, Strega herself!

It's easy to get here. There are two ferries a day which leave the port of Kaos at 5am and 7pm. The crossing takes about four hours. If you come over next week, you'll arrive in time for the Festival of the Magnotaur, which - I'm told - is not to be missed!

Look forward to seeing you!
Al

Here is the news at 6:30. This afternoon thieves stole the priceless Pipes of Paxi from Kaos Museum. The discovery of a red snake earring at the scene of the crime has led police to link the theft with the notorious gangsters and masters of disguise, Niagara Smith and Bronson Colt …

Strega and Lina on site - at lunch

Me outside Villa Magnotaur

Distress at Sea

The bus shuddered to a halt at the port. Nat grabbed his heavy backpack and stumbled out. He glanced at his watch and gulped. It was nearly seven o'clock – the Magnos ferry was due to leave any minute.

Nat dodged past a small dog and a man in a suit carrying armfuls of documents, and hurried down the dock to the ferry.

Suddenly Nat heard a shout. He turned to see the man in the suit wave at a boat. One of his documents lay flapping in the breeze behind him.

Nat dashed over and retrieved it. Close up, it looked just like an ordinary pink notebook – except for the writing on the cover. After an anxious glance at the ferry, he raced after the man.

The man was with two strange characters in funny white smocks and hats. They were deep in conversation and didn't notice Nat approach.

"Bad news from Hood," the man rasped. "The final cobra consignment has been held up in Enchillada. Take this lot straight to base. We'll keep Lamia informed about the movements of the …"

Nat cleared his throat. The man spun around and glared at him. Then he saw what was in Nat's hand.

"I'll take that!" he snapped. "Now push off, or else …"

His words were drowned by the blast of a ship's hooter. Nat looked up, horrorstruck. He was about to miss the ferry.

Three hours later, Nat wished he HAD missed the ferry. The boat heaved up and down as huge waves smashed against its sides. Lightning flashed overhead while passengers cowered miserably below deck.

The storm raged on and on. Was there any chance that the ferry was near Magnos? Nat struggled up onto the deck and stared out across the tossing sea, looking for signs of land.

A feeble light flickered ahead. He blinked as the light flashed again … and again. A distress signal!

The signal was obviously in Morse code. Quickly, Nat pulled out his notebook and jotted down the sequence of short and long flashes, using dots and dashes.

After the final flash, Nat desperately tried to decipher his scribbles. If only he could remember all of the Morse alphabet – not that it would be much help. The signal seemed to be in a foreign language …

Then it came to Nat in a flash. Of course! The message sent in Morse code must be in another code.

What does it say?

53

Ransacked!

Half an hour later, the storm vanished and the ferry chugged into the calm waters of Magnos port.

While Nat wandered up and down the waterfront, looking for Al, the Morse message whirred around in his head. It hadn't been a distress signal after all. But why had it been sent the wrong way around? And why did the name Lamia ring a faint bell?

Nat glanced anxiously at his watch. Another half hour had gone by and there was still no sign of Al. What had happened to him? Surely he hadn't forgotten that Nat was coming.

Shivering in the chilly night air, Nat decided to find his own way to Al's house, Villa Magnotaur. He checked the address on Al's letter, then headed up the steep hill into the town.

An hour and 57 wrong turns later, Nat stumbled down the steps from the top of the town wall, feeling very lost. As he scanned the rooftops, he spotted a tiny house with red tiles, half hidden by vines. He had found Villa Magnotaur at last!

Nat hurried down to the dimly lit street, raced through an arch and ran up a short flight of steps to the villa.

The door hung open … but once inside, Nat looked around in disbelief. The place had been ransacked. The contents of every cupboard and drawer had been tipped out, and Al was nowhere to be seen. Where was he? What was going on?

Among the debris, Nat caught sight of a symbol on a typed note. Where had he seen it before?

The note was addressed to someone called Taki. It contained a long list of directions to a rendezvous at Hotel Digitalis at eleven minutes past one, an odd time for a meeting … yet strangely familiar.

The note seemed to be Nat's only lead. He decided to go to the rendezvous. If Al wasn't there, Taki might know where he was.

Nat checked his watch. It was almost one o'clock. How would he ever reach the rendezvous in time? There had to be a short cut.

Luckily, a map of Magnos Town was lying on the floor, but none of the streets or hotels was named.

Where is Hotel Digitalis?
What is Nat's short cut?

Familiar Faces

A distant clock struck one as Nat shut the door and quickly slipped a note underneath, just in case Al turned up.

The short cut took much longer than Nat expected. Half an hour later, he had nearly reached Hotel Digitalis when he stopped dead. There were muffled voices ahead and they didn't sound friendly.

Nat hastily scrambled up a crumbling wall and stared at the strange scene in front of him.

A battered truck was parked outside the hotel, next to a boat. A sailor busily cleared the deck, while two familiar looking characters in white lowered the tailgate of the truck. All three were listening to a cloaked woman just below Nat.

"Hurry up and load the cargo," the woman snapped. "Once that's done Taki, go back to Villa Magnotaur and find that magazine. And don't mess up this time!"

"Meanwhile, Bron," she continued, "you must go straight to the meeting. The Medusa will return later to pick up the final consignment. Bogartus will fill you in with the details."

Nat watched the duo in white lug an enormous carpet out of the truck. Groaning under its weight, they staggered over to the boat. Just as they lowered their burden onto the deck, Nat glimpsed something hidden in its folds.

He leaned forward to take a closer look, missed his footing and crashed into a tangle of spiky bushes below.

The duo instantly dropped the carpet and dashed over to the wall, armed with flashlights.

"Hands up!" barked a woman. To Nat's surprise, the voice belonged to one of the characters in white. He crouched among the prickly leaves, not daring to move until she finally disappeared into the shadows.

Nat carefully extricated himself from his hiding place and darted over to a gateway, only to spot the sailor lurking under the arch.

In desperation he clambered up onto the wall. Suddenly he heard a shout behind him.

Quickly, he jumped down to the road, raced over to the truck and dived under a sheet of tarpaulin.

OUCH! Something sharp jabbed into Nat's hand. He held the object up to the glow from the rear light.

It was a snake shaped earring. Something about it jogged Nat's memory. He gasped in disbelief as it slowly dawned on him who the strange duo in white really were. So much for the masters of disguise!

Who are they?

To the Ancient City

Heavy footsteps stomped up to the truck. Trapped under the tarpaulin in the back, Nat held his breath as someone climbed into the cab. The engine wheezed uncertainly then roared to life. The truck lurched forward, then veered left up a steep, dusty track.

As the truck raced through the darkness, Nat tried to make sense of his latest discovery. Unlikely as it might seem, the couple in white were none other than the notorious gangsters, Niagara Smith and Bronson Colt! The duo were implicated in a theft from Kaos Museum. But what were they doing on Magnos ... and where was Al?

The truck bounded over a series of potholes then squealed to a halt. Nat peered out from under the tarpaulin and watched the bizarrely dressed figure of Bronson Colt clamber out, stare at a scrap of yellow paper, then scurry through an arch in a high wall. No one else was around, so Nat slipped out and tiptoed after him.

Hidden in the shadows, Nat followed the gangster down a long flight of steps and up some stairs to a balcony. Then the trail ran cold ...

MEHEHE! A goat was nibbling at Bronson's scrap of paper. Nat hastily rescued the fragment. He scanned its contents, then darted over to the edge of the balcony. The moonlight shone on the ruins of an ancient city below. This must be the site of Al's dig – and one of the ruined buildings was Bronson's mystery destination.

Which one?

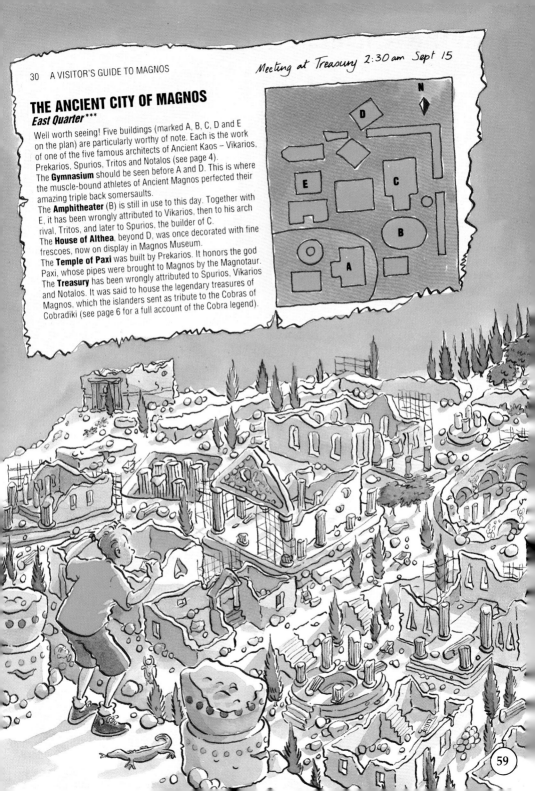

Meeting at Treasury 2:30 am Sept 15

THE ANCIENT CITY OF MAGNOS
*East Quarter***

Well worth seeing! Five buildings (marked A, B, C, D and E on the plan) are particularly worthy of note. Each is the work of one of the five famous architects of Ancient Kaos – Vikarios, Prekarios, Spurios, Tritos and Notalos (see page 4).

The **Gymnasium** should be seen before A and D. This is where the muscle-bound athletes of Ancient Magnos perfected their amazing triple back somersaults.

The **Amphitheater** (B) is still in use to this day. Together with E, it has been wrongly attributed to Vikarios, then to his arch rival, Tritos, and later to Spurios, the builder of C.

The **House of Althea**, beyond D, was once decorated with fine frescoes, now on display in Magnos Museum.

The **Temple of Paxi** was built by Prekarios. It honors the god Paxi, whose pipes were brought to Magnos by the Magnotaur.

The **Treasury** has been wrongly attributed to Spurios, Vikarios and Notalos. It was said to house the legendary treasures of Magnos, which the islanders sent as tribute to the Cobras of Cobradiki (see page 6 for a full account of the Cobra legend).

A Bizarre Meeting

Clutching Bronson's scrap of paper, Nat made his way to the ruined treasury.

He hauled himself up to a window and peered inside …

A bizarre meeting was in progress.

Fellow Cobras, the Head Cobra Lamia has decreed that we will gather in the throne room at sunset tomorrow. At the exact second that the Magnotaur Festival begins, Lamia will blow the Pipes of Paxi and Mount Ophis will awaken!

Once we have demonstrated our control over nature, we will demand that the islanders of Magnos send us, the Cobra gang, one million dollars each year, or else …

The meeting reached its creepy climax.

All hail to Lamia! All power to the Cobra gang!

While the strange crowd trooped out, two familiar figures waited behind.

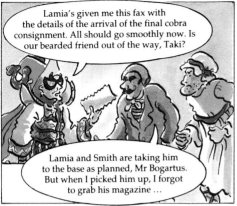

Lamia's given me this fax with the details of the arrival of the final cobra consignment. All should go smoothly now. Is our bearded friend out of the way, Taki?

Lamia and Smith are taking him to the base as planned, Mr Bogartus. But when I picked him up, I forgot to grab his magazine …

I went back to fetch it and found this! I don't know if the person who wrote it knew about the message in the star feature, but he'd certainly heard about the rendezvous at the hotel.

And then that wretched girl turned up …

First things first. Before the consignment arrives, we must decipher the message and find out where our bearded friend has hidden his information. As for the mystery letter writer, perhaps, with a little persuasion, the girl might tell us who he is. Where is she?

In the chest over there.

Let's get to work on her!

Nat had to distract them, quickly.

The sinister trio raced out.

Someone's watching us from that window. After him!

Nat unbolted the chest. As a dusty figure climbed out, his worst suspicions were confirmed …

Thanks!

He knew what had happened to Al.

What has happened to him? 61

Magazine Message

Al's assistant, Lina, brushed away a cobweb and gaped at Nat in disbelief as he introduced himself.

"How did you get here?" she asked. "Is Al with you? He arranged to meet me at the Temple of the Magnotaur at midnight. He said he was onto something but he never showed up, and when I went to look for him at Villa Magnotaur, I bumped into that thug called Taki."

Quickly, Nat told her everything he knew. From what he had heard and seen that night, he was certain that Al had been kidnapped by the strange crowd who called themselves the Cobra gang and smuggled aboard a boat bound for their base. But why?

"Perhaps he found out what those creeps are really up to," Lina suggested. "I can't believe all that baloney about the Pipes of Paxi."

Just then, Nat spotted a note in Al's writing. As he read it, Taki's odd conversation with the character called Mr Bogartus began to make sense.

"Al did have information after all," he said. "And he left Strega Nimbus a coded message in a magazine article revealing its hiding place. Thanks to Taki, the article's here, in front of us."

What does the message say?

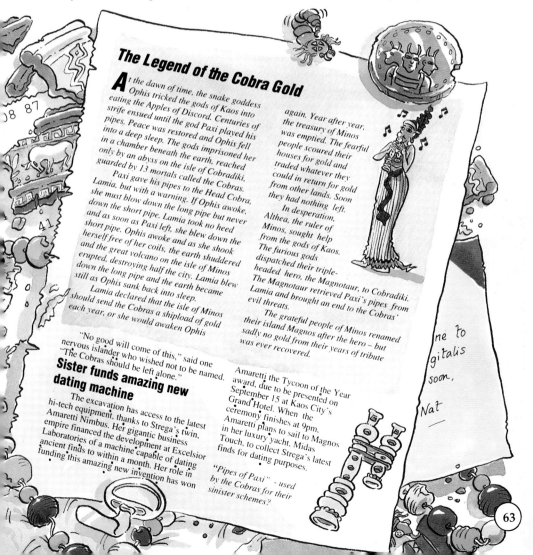

The Legend of the Cobra Gold

At the dawn of time, the snake goddess Ophis tricked the gods of Kaos into eating the Apples of Discord. Centuries of strife ensued until the god Paxi played his pipes. Peace was restored and Ophis fell into a deep sleep. The gods imprisoned her in a chamber beneath the earth, reached only by an abyss on the isle of Cobradiki, guarded by 13 mortals called the Cobras.

Paxi gave his pipes to the Head Cobra, Lamia, but with a warning. If Ophis awoke, she must blow down the long pipe but never down the short pipe. Lamia took no heed and as soon as Paxi left, she blew down the short pipe. Ophis awoke and as she shook herself free of her coils, the earth shuddered and the great volcano on the isle of Minos erupted, destroying half the city. Lamia blew down the long pipe and the earth became still as Ophis sank back into sleep.

Lamia declared that the isle of Minos should send the Cobras a shipload of gold each year, or she would awaken Ophis

again. Year after year, the treasury of Minos was emptied. The fearful people scoured their houses for gold and traded whatever they could in return for gold from other lands. Soon they had nothing left.

In desperation, Althea, the ruler of Minos, sought help from the gods of Kaos. The furious gods dispatched their triple-headed hero, the Magnotaur, to Cobradiki. The Magnotaur retrieved Paxi's pipes from Lamia and brought an end to the Cobras' evil threats.

The grateful people of Minos renamed their island Magnos after the hero – but sadly no gold from their years of tribute was ever recovered.

"No good will come of this," said one nervous islander who wished not to be named. "The Cobras should be left alone."

Sister funds amazing new dating machine

The excavation has access to the latest hi-tech equipment, thanks to Strega's twin, Amaretti Nimbus. Her gigantic business empire financed the development at Excelsior Laboratories of a machine capable of dating ancient finds to within a month. Her role in funding this amazing new invention has won

Amaretti the Tycoon of the Year award, due to be presented on September 15 at Kaos City's Grand Hotel. When the ceremony finishes at 9pm, Amaretti plans to sail to Magnos in her luxury yacht, Midas Touch, to collect Strega's latest finds for dating purposes.

"Pipes of Paxi" – used by the Cobras for their sinister schemes?

ne to
gitalis
soon,

Nat

Clifftop Chase

Suddenly an angry shout rang out across the ruined treasury. Nat looked over his shoulder and gulped as he saw Bogartus and his two henchmen, ready to pounce.

"I'll take these," Lina cried, grabbing Bogartus's fax and a carved stone. "Follow me!"

She darted past the villainous trio and sprinted outside. With Bronson's bloodcurdling threats ringing in his ears, Nat hurried after her.

His mind whirled as he ran. What if Bronson and his pals had based themselves on the Cobras in the magazine article? They had stolen the Pipes of Paxi … Could they also be behind the theft from Strega's safe?

Lina raced along the cliff ahead. Then, to Nat's horror, she suddenly disappeared over the edge.

"We've got you," Bronson growled behind him. "You'll regret you ever meddled with the Cobra gang."

Taking a deep breath, Nat swung himself down the rockface. For one long second, he dangled in midair … until his right foot finally hit a ledge.

"Now move your left foot down …"

Nat almost fell off the cliff when he heard Lina's voice in the darkness below. Following her whispered instructions, he inched his way to the bottom. When he stepped onto the shore, he looked up in disbelief at an ornate doorway carved into the rock.

"Welcome to the Temple of the Magnotaur!" Lina smiled. "Sorry about the short cut. Come on in."

Al's information was hidden under the massive altar stone. To move the stone, they had to press Thebe's right eye then Alexi's left eye. Nat stared at a crumbling fresco on the far wall. Were Thebe and Alexi among the bizarre painted figures? Perhaps the strange symbols held the answer.

Can you identify Thebe and Alexi?

Vital Information

Nat and Lina each pressed a painted eye, then watched the altar stone expectantly. For a moment, nothing happened, then, with a low grinding sound, the huge stone slid away to reveal a secret compartment.

Nat eagerly reached inside and fished out Al's diary. Hidden in its pages were some scraps of paper, two photos and a tattered parchment scroll. While Lina examined the scroll, Nat flipped to the last entry in the diary and began to read.

...to VM at dusk ...left my key in the Treasury. When I reached the ruin, I heard voices inside.

Peered around the doorway and spotted a character in a cloak with a sailor and a businessman. I remember every word of their strange conversation.

"By the Pipes of Paxi, that machine will be ready tomorrow, Mr. Bogartus," the sailor promised. "Except for the laser mechanism, of course."

"I should hope so too," the businessman snapped. "The laser components arrive in Kaos tomorrow. Niagara and Bronson will collect them, then pick up Lamia and yourself from Magnos Old Port at eleven minutes past one before heading for base. Then it's up to you to make sure that the laser mechanism is ready by Saturday – or else."

"What if the Enchilladan airport strike goes ahead?" the sailor asked. "The crystal will never reach us in time."

"Enough of your excuses!" the businessman snorted. "The trial run of the laser mechanism must go ahead on

Saturday. If Mt Ophis erupts as planned, then the rest of the machine will be activated and the next phase of our project shall begin."

He turned to his pal in the cloak and said something I could catch, then they left the building. While retrieving my key, I found some scraps of paper – and one of S's stolen scrolls! Luckily I took photos of the trio with my new camera. Must show them to S and tell her everything tomorrow.

Fri 14
S felt we should find out what's going on before contacting the police. She suggested that I hide her scroll, together with diary, photos and scraps of paper, and tell her where to find them in case anything should happen. S volunteered to go to Old Port tonight. Arranged to meet at her house at 8.30 tomorrow morning to figure out our next move.

Must tell L where to find diary if worst happens to me or S!

Remove gold from secret chamber and store in cellar of Hotel Digitalis. To enter secret chamber, press five buttons in order – symbols on 1st, 2nd and 5th are the same – symbols on 3rd and 4th also match – 3rd is two buttons directly above 1st, but isn't in top row – 2nd is two buttons directly below 4th – 5th is next to 4th and in same row.

Bogartus
Director
Fax 0202 08 87

KAOTIK CRUISES
TAKI: HOTEL HADES, KAOS

"Look at these," Nat said, passing Lina the photos. "This is proof that Bogartus and Taki were behind the theft from Strega's safe, and …"

He gasped in horror as a massive figure in a billowing white smock loomed in front of them. It was Bronson Colt! How had he got here?

"Hand over that diary," Bronson snarled. "Hurry up! There's no escape this time."

Impatiently, he wrenched the diary from Nat's shaking hands. Then, to Nat's dismay, he ripped it apart, struck a match and set fire to the pages.

"Ha ha, you'll never pin anything on us now," the villain gloated as charred fragments of paper floated up from the flames.

"You've forgotten something!" Lina cried, waving the photos at him. "What about these? And here's half of someone's business card too …"

Bronson dived at her, but she nimbly skipped aside. With a bellow of fury, he tripped into the trench in front of the altar. Quickly Lina ran for the doorway. Bronson shoved Nat aside and charged after her.

"Find Strega!" Lina yelled at Nat. "She lives in the big house on Paxi Square. Explain what's happened. I'll see you later."

Nat dashed outside, blinking in the bright morning light, and began to run along the shore to Magnos Town.

The Plot Thickens

At last, Magnos Town came into view. Gasping for breath, Nat raced along the narrow stretch of sand, determined to reach Strega's house and summon help.

As Nat reached the bustling waterfront, a strong smell of fish hit his nostrils. Last night's catch had been unloaded and Magnos's fish market was in full swing.

Nat dodged past swooping seagulls and traders with crates of sardines, and found a sign to Paxi Square.

Minutes later, he stumbled up a steep lane into a large, dusty square. Behind the high railings in front of him stood a grand, but slightly shabby house. Although it was morning, its peeling shutters were still firmly closed.

Nat ran up to the door and tugged the bell pull. A series of bells clanged wildly through the house then there was silence. As he waited, a cold feeling crept down his spine. Had something happened to Strega?

Nat pushed the door gently. To his surprise, it swung open, revealing a long hall.

"Hello there!" he cried. His voice echoed through the house, but there was no answer.

Then he spotted half of a torn business card lying on the marble floor. It looked all too familiar!

When Nat had a closer look, his worst fears were confirmed.

R-R-RING! Nat jumped as the shrill sound of a telephone cut through the silence. He thundered upstairs, dashed across a shadowy room and grabbed the receiver, but the phone went dead.

Nat wrenched open the shutters and the morning sunlight streamed inside. He was in Strega's study.

He picked up an official looking document. As he read its contents, the truth slowly dawned on him. The Cobra legend, the Pipes of Paxi, the bizarre costumes … all these were side issues. Central to the Cobra gang's sinister plot was the safe arrival of the final COBRA consignment.

What is the final consignment?

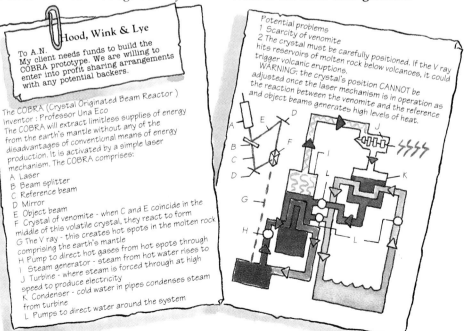

Hood, Wink & Lye

To A.N.
My client needs funds to build the COBRA prototype. We are willing to enter into profit sharing arrangements with any potential backers.

The COBRA (Crystal Originated Beam Reactor)
Inventor : Professor Una Eco
The COBRA will extract limitless supplies of energy from the earth's mantle without any of the disadvantages of conventional means of energy production. It is activated by a simple laser mechanism. The COBRA comprises:

A Laser
B Beam splitter
C Reference beam
D Mirror
E Object beam
F Crystal of venomite - when C and E coincide in the middle of this volatile crystal, they react to form hot spots in the molten rock
G The V ray - this creates hot spots in the molten rock comprising the earth's mantle
H Pump to direct hot gases from hot spots through
I Steam generator - steam from hot water rises to
J Turbine - where steam is forced through at high speed to produce electricity
K Condenser - cold water in pipes condenses steam from turbine
L Pumps to direct water around the system

Potential problems
1 Scarcity of venomite
2 The crystal must be carefully positioned. If the V ray hits reservoirs of molten rock below volcanoes, it could trigger volcanic eruptions.
WARNING: the crystal's position CANNOT be adjusted once the laser mechanism is in operation as the reaction between the venomite and the reference and object beams generates high levels of heat.

A Secret Cipher

As Nat examined the rest of the papers, a dark figure appeared in the doorway … It was Lina.

"We've got to get out of here," she gasped. "That thug in the smock is heading straight for the house!"

The duo raced downstairs only to discover Bronson blocking the front door. Quickly, they turned and fled down the corridor into the garden.

"You'll regret this!" Bronson panted, close behind.

Lina scrambled over the garden wall and landed with a squelch on a crate of grapes in a cart below.

Just as Nat swung himself down, the driver cracked his whip and the cart pulled away. Lina hastily grabbed Nat and hauled him aboard.

"Where's Strega?" she asked as the cart creaked and swayed down the narrow street.

"It looks like the worst has happened," Nat said, producing the torn card. "Somehow, Bogartus and Co. discovered that Strega knew about the COBRA machine."

Nat quickly explained to Lina what the COBRA was. From what he had read in Al's diary, he was convinced that the crooks had built the machine at their base, using components smuggled from Kaos. All they needed now was one vital crystal of venomite.

"Remember the stolen gem called the Serpent's Eye of Enchillada?" he said. "I suspect that it is their final consignment. Once the gem arrives, the gang will activate the machine's laser mechanism and make Mount Ophis erupt, then threaten further eruptions unless Magnos pays up."

"Just like the Cobras in the legend," Lina said. "But what was all that talk about the powers of the Pipes of Paxi at the meeting, and why was …?"

The cart rattled to a halt on the waterfront. Nat and Lina jumped off and dived into a cafe. Munching their way through a pile of sticky pastries, they discussed their next move.

"We've got to intercept the final consignment," Nat said. "It arrives on Magnos today, but we don't know where or when."

"All the details are here, in Bogartus's fax," Lina said, fishing out a torn strip of paper. "There's just one snag – they're in a secret code."

Nat rummaged in his pocket and pulled out a similar strip, together with a grid and a list of words.

"I found these among the papers at Strega's house," he explained.

Nat's strip of paper was covered with meaningless numbers, but unlike Bogartus's fax, someone had added letters which formed a clear message. If they could figure out how the cipher worked, they might be able to decode the secret details of the final consignment's arrival.

What does Bogartus's fax say?

The Final Consignment

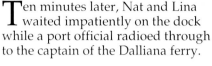

I've had a tip-off. My informers believe that a passenger called Ophis has the stolen Serpent's Eye of Enchillada.

Ten minutes later, Nat and Lina waited impatiently on the dock while a port official radioed through to the captain of the Dalliana ferry.

Their hearts sank as the reply crackled through. There was no one called Ophis on the boat. The official shrugged and hurried away as the Dalliana chugged slowly into port.

Nat watched the passengers trickle onto the dock. Two men in dark suits pushed their way through the brightly dressed crowd. Nat instantly recognized the man he had met at the port of Kaos. But who was his sinister sidekick?

The man glanced furtively over his shoulder. He muttered something to his pal and they began to run. Nat raced after them, but it was hopeless. The shady duo leaped aboard a boat which had pulled up by the dock, unnoticed. It was the villains' boat, the Medusa! With a deafening roar, the boat spun around and sped out to sea.

They're over there!

"Ahoy there!" cried Lina. She sat at the helm of a small motorboat and revved the engine impatiently. "It's Al's boat. Jump aboard!"

They trailed the Medusa across the shimmering sea to two rocky islets. Just as the crooks disappeared behind a barren headland, the boat's engine spluttered ominously, shuddered, then went dead.

Lina struggled to restart the motor, but there was not even the faintest spark of life.

"We must have run out of fuel," she groaned. "We'll have to paddle."

The boat tilted precariously as she rummaged for a pair of oars. Soon they were ready to set off.

"Which way?" Lina asked, producing a small chart.

Nat thought hard. The crooks must be heading for their secret base. If the gang had based itself on the legendary Cobras, surely its HQ would be on the island of Cobradiki. But Cobradiki wasn't on Lina's chart … unless its name had changed.

Where should they go?

It's a little temperamental.

Into the Base

Four hot and exhausting hours later, Nat sighted the Medusa at the foot of a steep, forbidding cliff. The blazing sun beat down on them as they rowed over to investigate.

Lina led the way up a flight of steps carved into the rock. Snakes basked in the heat, ignoring her as she carefully crept past.

"So the Cobra part of the legend is true after all," Lina gasped, when she finally reached the top.

Out of a huge crater below rose a vast ancient palace. Golden serpents glittered above its doorways. This had to be the Cobra gang's base.

"We've got to grab the Serpent's Eye before they activate the COBRA machine," Nat said. "According to Bogartus, they're meeting in the throne room at sunset. That must be where they've built the machine … and where we will find the Eye."

Lina pulled out the scroll and the stone that she had picked up earlier. With the help of these objects, they could locate the throne room and figure out which of the entrances below would lead them there.

Where should they enter the palace?

Prisoners in the Labyrinth

They were only two rooms away from their goal when Nat raced around a corner and ran straight into Bronson. Then everything went black.

When Nat came to, he breathed in cold, musty air. A dazzling light shone in his eyes. He blinked and saw Lina. Suddenly his watch bleeped six. He jumped to his feet. The Serpent's Eye! They had to find it before the gang activated the COBRA machine.

"There's just one snag," Lina said, puzzling over the plan of the palace. "I can't figure out where we are."

She ran down a long, dark passage and turned left into another passage. This led to a flight of steps going down into yet another passage. Nat sprinted after her, not noticing the shadowy figure closing behind him … until it was too late.

Lina turned and looked on in horror, as Nat struggled in the clutches of a huge stranger …

"Nat!" exclaimed a friendly voice. "And Lina too! What are you doing here? What's going on?"

Nat sighed with relief. This was no stranger – it was Al! Al looked dazed as Nat quickly explained what had happened and told him about the Cobra gang's sinister plot.

"And we've got to stop them before it's too late," cried Lina, disappearing up a flight of stairs. "Come on!"

She turned left at the top. Nat and Al followed her down a strange, twisting passage to a dead end.

"Wait!" she gasped, before they could retrace their steps.

On the wall ahead was a painting of a huge maze. With the help of her carved stone, Lina swiftly translated the symbols above it.

"So this is the legendary labyrinth of Ophis," Al said, awestruck. "It was built beneath the Cobras' palace to confuse Ophis if she ever escaped from the abyss … so the story goes."

"And we must be trapped somewhere in the middle," Nat groaned, thinking back to his journey along the darkened passages.

"There's an entrance to the labyrinth from the palace," Lina piped up. "It's marked on the plan with a sign that matches one of the symbols on the painting. It's probably bolted and barred, but it's our only hope."

What is their route to the entrance?

In Search of the COBRA

Luckily for the trio, the trapdoor to the palace was unbolted. Nat, Lina and Al squeezed through the tiny opening and scrambled up into a deserted hall.

"I hope it's not too far to the throne room," Al gulped, looking anxiously at the fading light.

"This way," Lina cried, running over to a grand marble staircase.

As they reached the throne room at the top of the stairs, Nat groaned in despair. They were too late. The gang had already assembled … and there was no sign of the COBRA machine.

None of the bizarrely dressed crooks noticed the horrified trio at the entrance. They were listening intently to a ridiculous masked figure on a podium in front of the throne. It was Bogartus in all his glory.

"Cobras, be vigilant," he declared. "A prisoner is on the loose. But she can't stop us from fulfilling our destiny. By the Pipes of Paxi, Ophis will reawaken and Magnos shall pay us tribute once more!"

What prisoner? Could he mean Strega? Nat saw one tiny glimmer of hope. But where was the COBRA machine? And why weren't all the gangsters at the meeting?

"Watch out," Al hissed, grabbing Nat and Lina. "We've got company."

He dragged them behind a pillar as three more costumed characters swept up the stairway. The leader carried the Pipes of Paxi. Surely this was Lamia, the Head Cobra. Nat instantly recognized her surly attendants.

The three villains paraded into the throne room, then the doors thudded shut and bolts were rammed into place. What could they do now?

"Look at this," Lina gasped, pulling out the ancient plan. "The throne room is twice the size of the room we've just seen and there's a door at each end!"

Why wasn't the COBRA machine in the throne room? Why should the gang want to hide it from view? Nat's mind buzzed with questions as he raced after the others. But when they reached the place where a door was marked on the plan, there was only a painted wall.

"What's happened to the door?" Lina muttered, scratching her head. "It's definitely on the plan."

While Al poked and prodded the wall in search of hidden levers, Nat spotted a panel of buttons to the right.

Buttons! Nat's mind flashed back to a scrap of paper tucked inside Al's diary. It had contained details of a sequence of buttons. If he could remember the sequence, they might find a way inside the hidden room.

Which buttons should Nat press?

Sabotage

As Nat pressed the final button, the wall slid back to reveal an incredible contraption. It had to be the COBRA machine. High up among the fanbelts sparkled a giant crystal.

"The Serpent's Eye!" Nat yelled, charging up a flight of stairs. "We've got to reach it before they start the machine, or it will be too late!"

"Watch out," Al panted behind him. "There's trouble ahead."

Nat looked up and gulped. Two burly figures were lurking at the top. A third man crouched in the shadows by the crystal.

"Not so fast!" Taki growled, brandishing a large spanner.

The next second the two thugs pounced. Nat darted out of their way, ducked under a row of fanbelts and raced over to the crystal. But he had forgotten the third man.

"Grab him, Zither!" cried Taki.

The man sprang at him. Quickly, Nat jumped onto a nearby ladder. As he clambered up past more pulleys and cogs, a plan began to form in his head. Maybe he didn't have to remove the Serpent's Eye after all …

Zither lunged for his ankle, but Nat kicked himself free and staggered up onto a platform. His head swam as he looked down into the throne room far below. He was about to steady himself on a cable when he saw that it was connected to some kind of lever next to the Head Cobra's throne.

Just then, Nat noticed three handles to his right. If he turned just one handle, he could sabotage the gang's fiendish scheme … but what would happen if he chose the wrong one?

"O Ophis awake!" cried a woman's voice, echoing up into the hidden room. "Wreak vengeance on Magnos!"

"You're too late," Zither jeered at Nat, as he scrambled up onto the platform. "You'll never stop us now!"

As a long, shrill note blasted through the air, Nat's brain leaped into action. He had only seconds left to make his vital decision.

Which handle should he turn?

The Palace of Doom

With a gleeful cry, Zither pushed Nat aside and spun all three handles back.

"The laser is still in activation mode," he gloated. "Your feeble sabotage attempt has failed!"

"Not so!" Al panted at the top of the ladder. "As soon as Nat disabled the laser, I grabbed the crystal."

Zither's howls of rage were drowned by an ominous rumbling deep below. Suddenly the whole palace shuddered and foul smelling smoke filled the air. Lina hastily scrambled onto the platform, with Taki and his sinister pal close behind.

BOOM! Everyone dived for cover as a massive explosion ripped through the hidden room.

As twisted machinery flew through the air, Zither and his terrified cronies dashed across the platform, seized the cable attached to the Head Cobra's lever and slithered down into the throne room below.

As another tremor rocked the palace, Nat staggered over to the cable. Luckily it was still firmly secured above … but for how long?

With chunks of the building raining down on them, the trio abseiled into the throne room. But a figure in a mask was waiting below. Al hung helplessly in midair as Lamia tried to snatch the crystal out of his hand.

"Look out!" cried Lina, as a giant pillar crashed to the ground, narrowly missing the Head Cobra.

Seized by panic, the gangsters raced to the doors, wrenched back the bolts and stampeded outside.

"Flee!" someone shrieked. "It's the revenge of Ophis!"

The villains disappeared through a hole in the palace's outer wall. The next second, the entire wall collapsed in a mountain of rubble.

Not everyone had escaped. By the entrance to the labyrinth, Lina spotted Lamia's hat and the Pipes of Paxi. A fax and an ancient scroll lay nearby.

A familiar sign leaped into focus. In a flash, Lina realized that Lamia knew a safe route out of the doomed palace. The vital details were in front of them. They had to find it – and fast.

What is the safe route?

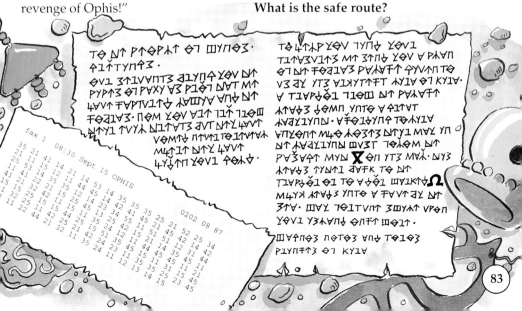

Farewell Cobradiki

Ahoy there!

HELP!

Twenty terrifying minutes later, Nat, Lina and Al staggered out of a cave onto the shore. Dark clouds of smoke rolled down the cliff and huge waves smashed against the rocks.

Through the spray, Nat spotted a boat heading out to sea. They frantically tried to attract its attention, but their cries were drowned by a deep roar coming from the very heart of the island.

Just as the trio lost hope, the boat turned back. As it approached, Nat's heart sank. It was the Medusa …

"Don't worry!" a cheerful voice cried from the cabin. "Just jump in the back and I'll get us out of here."

They scrambled aboard and sped away from the doomed island.

Suddenly there was a deafening BOOM. A fiery light flashed across the sky, then chunks of molten rock and red hot lava shot through the air.

"So the island was a dormant volcano," said Al. "Its vent must have been directly below the room where the gang built the machine. But why has it erupted now?"

Nat thought hard. Could the laser have triggered the eruption without the Serpent's Eye? Or did the Pipes of Paxi have mysterious powers after all?

"There's someone in the water!" Lina yelled, pointing at a flailing figure in the distance.

The Medusa swiftly turned and headed back across the churning sea. As the boat drew closer, Al threw the stricken stranger a line. She caught it and swam weakly up to the side. Al helped her aboard, while Nat and Lina dashed into the cabin in search of towels and dry clothes.

All they could find were two grubby rags and a half empty bottle of strong Magnotaur liquor. When Nat emerged back on deck, Al was listening sympathetically to the bedraggled stranger's sad tale.

"… and when I returned home, they were waiting for me," she said. "Then everything went black."

"I came to in some kind of labyrinth," the stranger continued. "As I began to search for a way out, the tremors started …"

She clutched at her cloak and shivered. CRASH! Nat dropped the liquor bottle in surprise.

"It's a pack of lies from beginning to end," he cried. "Don't believe a word of it!"

Why not?

The COBRA Project

Strega Nimbus, alias Lamia, sprang to her feet and pointed a pistol at the horrified trio.

"Hands up!" she hissed. "Give me the Serpent's Eye, quickly."

Al reluctantly reached into his pocket and pulled out the crystal. As the last rays of the sun flashed across the gem, Strega paused. She did not notice the figure on the cabin roof, unfurling a large, flapping sail until …

Strega cried out in fury as the heavy sail descended on her, knocking the pistol from her grasp. It fell into the water with a small plop.

"Good riddance!" a cheerful voice cried as the gun disappeared from view.

"Professor Eco!" gasped Nat, glimpsing her face for the first time. "How did you get here?"

"It's a long story," the missing scientist began. "I was looking for funds to build my invention, the COBRA, when I received a letter from someone called Ophis. This person offered to help me if I followed their orders and kept the project secret."

"I believed that my invention would be used to benefit humankind," Eco continued. "So I accepted the proposal. I staged my disappearance and built the COBRA, using parts supplied by Taki."

"I realized that something fishy was going on when Taki brought me the Serpent's Eye," she said. "I made my escape through the labyrinth. I knew which way to go as I had laid pipes through its passages to supply the machine with sea water."

"I found this boat by the cliff," the professor went on. "I met the Magnos fishing fleet when the tremors began. We reached the island in time to pick up Taki and his cronies. They were glad to see us! Now they're on their way to Magnos jail."

Smiling, Eco pointed at a small fleet of boats in the distance. But Nat knew that it was not time to celebrate yet. According to the fax that Lina had found in the Cobras' palace, one big time crook was still at large, known only by the codename, Ophis.

"Look what our friends left behind!" Lina said, popping out of the cabin with a pink notebook. "Perhaps this contains Ophis's true identity."

Nat recognized it instantly. It was the document that he had picked up at the port of Kaos the day before and returned to Zither without ever glancing at its contents.

As Nat read the first pages, everything began to fall into place. At last he knew why Bronson and Niagara had stolen the Pipes of Paxi, and why Bogartus had spun the yarn about their mythical powers.

Most of the gangsters had never known about the COBRA machine. They were just a smokescreen for the operations of a far more sinister outfit.

The pages did not reveal Ophis's name, but Nat had enough to go on. He glanced at his watch. It was 8:30 already. Time was running out …

Who is Ophis?

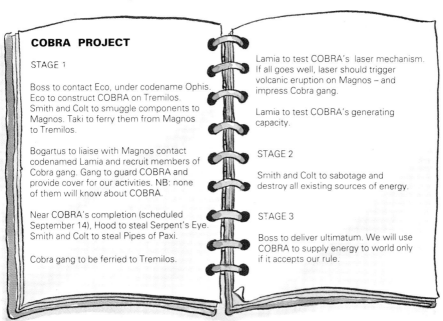

COBRA PROJECT

STAGE 1

Boss to contact Eco, under codename Ophis. Eco to construct COBRA on Tremilos. Smith and Colt to smuggle components to Magnos. Taki to ferry them from Magnos to Tremilos.

Bogartus to liaise with Magnos contact codenamed Lamia and recruit members of Cobra gang. Gang to guard COBRA and provide cover for our activities. NB: none of them will know about COBRA.

Near COBRA's completion (scheduled September 14), Hood to steal Serpent's Eye. Smith and Colt to steal Pipes of Paxi.

Cobra gang to be ferried to Tremilos.

Lamia to test COBRA's laser mechanism. If all goes well, laser should trigger volcanic eruption on Magnos – and impress Cobra gang.

Lamia to test COBRA's generating capacity.

STAGE 2

Smith and Colt to sabotage and destroy all existing sources of energy.

STAGE 3

Boss to deliver ultimatum. We will use COBRA to supply energy to world only if it accepts our rule.

Cobra Gold

BANG! Hundreds of brilliant lights exploded across the dark skies above Magnos.

"The Magnotaur Festival's begun!" Lina whooped. "We've arrived just in time for the firework display."

While Al and Eco moored the boat, Nat and Lina searched the happy dancing crowds for the port official. Strega and the rest of the Cobra gang were safely in the back of a police van, but Ophis was still at large. She was due to leave the port of Kaos any moment now. This sinister crook had to be stopped, before she escaped from the clutches of the law.

"You've got to believe us this time!" Lina insisted, as the official listened to them sceptically. "We'll explain later."

While he radioed through to his colleagues in Kaos, Al and Eco raced down the waterfront carrying two mysterious bundles.

"Long live the Magnotaur!" they cried, plonking two sets of festival horns on Nat's and Lina's heads.

"Although the Magnotaur is obviously a myth," Al added, then ducked hastily as a stray firework whizzed past his left ear.

"Or rather, he was really three people called Magnos, Notos and Toros," he continued. "But the Cobra Gold must be a legend. No one's ever found a trace of it …"

"Strega did," Lina said. "She discovered that the ancient Cobras stored the gold in the secret chamber behind the throne room."

"What happened to it?" asked Eco, puzzled. "I never saw any gold there when I was building the COBRA."

"I know where it is," Nat grinned.

Where is the Cobra Gold?

STAR IN COBRA CONSPIRACY

SU SPURIOS, Chief Reporter

STREGA NIMBUS, star of "Battlestar Elektra", played a leading role in the Cobra conspiracy, it emerged yesterday.

There was uproar in the courtroom when Strega Nimbus was unmasked as the leader of the Cobra gang. This organization aimed to extort vast sums of money from the island of Magnos. Members included top executives from the Hudlum City company, Sci Fi Inc, and the notorious gangsters, Niagara Smith and Bronson Colt.

STAR TURNS LOOTER

Ms. Nimbus was also charged with looting the treasures of Magnos, the so-called Cobra Gold, from the island of Tremilos. It was alleged that she plotted to sell the treasures through a firm of Hudlum City art dealers.

How the Cobra gang intended to force Magnos into handing over its millions remains a mystery. Speculation has been fueled by the trial of a person, identified only as X. The press were not admitted to the proceedings which were held in conditions of top secrecy.

Villa Magnotaur
Magnotaur Passage
Town Wall
Magnos Town

Dear Nat,

Here are the photos I promised you, together with some newspaper clippings. I hope they make interesting reading! Notice there's no mention of a certain machine. It's all been hushed up.

I've just received a letter from Eco. She's returned the Serpent's Eye to the Geological Society of Enchillada. The Enchilladans are very grateful and they've invited you, me and Lina over to Enchillada next month to be presented with a small reward.

Meanwhile Lina and I are still busily assessing the Cobra Gold. With the help of the new dating machine at Excelsior Laboratories, we've discovered that some of the treasures are 3,999 years old! And you'd never guess, a team of Enchilladan geologists has just found evidence of a volcanic eruption on Magnos exactly 4,000 years ago. No wonder the poor islanders paid up!

See you soon,

Al

MYSTERY DISAPPEARANCE OF TYCOON OF THE YEAR

AMARETTI NIMBUS of Sci Fi Inc vanished in mysterious circumstances after receiving the TYCOON OF THE YEAR award at Kaos City's Grand Hotel.

The SFI boss won the award for funding Excelsior Laboratories' hi-tech dating machine. She was last seen speeding off to the port of Kaos in her limousine.

Amaretti with award

STOLEN PIPES RETURN TO MUSEUM

Leading archeologist Al Rose and his assistant Lina Rebus present the Pipes of Paxi to Professor Kurios, curator of Kaos Museum. The priceless pipes were stolen last month by Niagara Smith and Bronson Colt of the Cobra gang. Latest developments in the Cobra conspiracy trial on p.3.

Clues

Pages 52-53

Is this really a code? Try reading the message in reverse order. You'll find it easier to identify the missing letters.

Pages 54-55

Start by locating Villa Magnotaur on the map. Look carefully at the villa and try tracing Taki's route there.

Pages 56-57

Remember the 6:30 news.

Pages 58-59

Match up the ruins with the plan, then identify them by a process of elimination. What do you know about the Treasury? What are C and E?

Pages 60-61

Do you know who Bogartus's "bearded friend" could be? Where have you seen Taki's note before? Who is the girl?

Pages 62-63

Try writing down the letters with dots below them in groups of six.

Pages 64-65

Do you know the legend of the Cobra Gold? Can you identify two characters and a musical instrument? Could the symbols next to them be their names in an ancient script?

Pages 68-69

Think back to Al's diary. Did you notice the news clipping in Villa Magnotaur?

Pages 70-71

How does L become 34 on the decoded fax? Bogartus's fax uses a different keyword.

Pages 72-73

Think back to the fresco and remember the magazine article. Cobradiki may not be the only island that has changed its name.

Pages 74-75

If you're familiar with the symbols on the fresco, you can translate the inscriptions on the stone. Now decipher the writing on the scroll. This is a three dimensional maze.

Pages 76-77

Start by tracing Nat and Lina's route before they bumped into Al.

Pages 78-79

Which row is the third button in? Look at the symbols in that row – what happens if the symbol on the third button is a triangle?

Pages 80-81

Remember the COBRA papers in Strega's study. How is the V Ray formed? Try matching up the diagram with the machine.

Pages 82-83

The stone will prove handy here.

Pages 84-85

Where has Nat seen her before?

Pages 86-87

Have you decoded the fax which Lina found in the palace. Think back to the magazine article.

Page 88

Look at the latest fax. Do you remember the white scrap of paper in Al's diary?

Answers

Pages 52-53

The Morse signal is not in another code. It has just been sent in reverse order. With the missing letters added, it says:

MEDUSA – RENDEZVOUS AT MAGNOS OLD PORT AT 01:11 AS PREVIOUSLY ARRANGED – LAMIA

Pages 54-55

First, Nat has to locate Villa Magnotaur by recalling his own route there. The villa is up a short passage across a street, opposite the steps to the top of the town wall (see page 54). There are two places on the map which match this location. Nat can figure out which is the correct location by following Taki's directions from Styx Street to the villa in reverse order. Now he can trace Taki's route from Villa Magnotaur to Hotel Digitalis, via Hotel Hydra. This is marked in black. Nat's short cut is shown in red.

Hotel Digitalis   Styx Street

Hotel Hydra   Villa Magnotaur

Pages 56-57

All the evidence suggests that the strange duo are the notorious gangsters and masters of disguise, Niagara Smith and Bronson Colt.

When Nat spots the duo by the truck outside Hotel Digitalis, one of them (a woman) is wearing a red S shaped earring, but in the next picture it is missing. This must be the red snake earring that Nat finds in the truck. An identical earring was mentioned on the 6:30 news (page 51). Its discovery after a theft from Kaos Museum led police to link the crime with Smith and Colt.

The instructions on the typed note on page 55 mention "Rendezvous with S and C at 01:11 at Hotel Digitalis". Could S and C be Smith and Colt?

Finally, the cloaked woman addressed someone outside the hotel as "Bron". Could this be short for Bronson Colt?

Pages 58-59

According to the handwritten message on the scrap of paper, there is a meeting at the Treasury. This must be where Bronson is going. The scrap is from a guide book and it reveals that the Treasury is in the East Quarter of the ancient city of Magnos. When you compare the plan on the scrap of paper with the view from the balcony, you will see that the Treasury must be one of the ruins below.

(continued)

Pages 58-59 (continued)

If you match up the plan with the ruins, you can locate the Treasury by a process of elimination. According to the scrap of paper, the Treasury was not built by Spurios, Vikarios or Notalos, or by Prekarios, who built the Temple of Paxi, so it must have been built by Tritos. The Treasury cannot be B, which is the Amphitheater, or C, which was built by Spurios, or E, which was wrongly attributed to Tritos. This means that it must be A or D.

Before you can find out which one is the Treasury, you have to identify E and C. The Amphitheater (B) was not built by Tritos, Spurios, Prekarios or Vikarios, so its builder must be Notalos. E was not

This is the Treasury.

built by Tritos, Vikarios or Spurios, and now you know it was not built by Notalos, so its builder must be Prekarios and it must be the Temple of Paxi. The Gymnasium is not A, B or D, and it cannot be E, so it must be C.

The House of Althea is not D, and it cannot be B, C or E. This means that it must be A and the Treasury must be D.

Pages 60-61

Al must have been kidnapped by Taki and taken to the Cobra gang's base. All the evidence points this way.

At the bizarre meeting, the man in the mask called Mr. Bogartus is talking about "our bearded friend". Think back to Al's photo (page 51). Could this person be Al?

The note that Taki found when he returned to the mystery person's house looks familiar. It is the note that Nat left under Al's door on page 56. It looks like Taki picked up the "bearded friend"from Villa Magnotaur.

When the girl who bumped into Taki after he found Nat's note turns out to be Al's assistant, Lina, it is obvious that Taki was at Villa Magnotaur.

This all fits in with Taki's movements before the meeting. Remember his instructions on the typed note (page 55) and the cloaked woman's orders (page 56). Could Al have been his "cargo"?

Pages 62-63

The letters with dots below them form this message:

OGTOELPMETOFRUATONGAMANDSSER
PTHEBESTHGIREYENEHTALEXISTFELE
YEOTMOVERATLASTONEDNAFINDNOIT
AMROFNI

Starting with the first word, every alternate word has been written in reverse. Decoded, the message says:

GO TO TEMPLE OF MAGNOTAUR AND PRESS THEBE'S RIGHT EYE THEN ALEXI'S LEFT EYE TO MOVE ALTAR STONE AND FIND INFORMATION

Pages 64-65

Thinking back to the legend of the Cobra Gold (page 63), the three headed man in the fresco must be the Magnotaur. In the right hand painting, there are nine symbols above his neck. Could these spell "Magnotaur" in an ancient script? Except for G, N and U, the symbols are similar to their corresponding letters in the modern alphabet. Using "Magnotaur" as a key, together with your knowledge of the legend, you can translate the symbols above the other people in the right hand painting as "Lamia and the Cobras" and the symbols below the musical pipes as "the Pipes of Paxi". Now you can decode most of the symbols on the fresco and deduce what the remaining symbols must be. This is what they say:

IN FRONT OF PRINCE NIOBE AND PRINCESS THEBE, ALTHEA OF MINOS VOWS TO PROTECT THE PIPES OF PAXI AND USE THEM ONLY IF OPHIS SHOULD AWAKEN AGAIN.

AT THE PALACE OF THE GODS ON THE ISLE OF KIRA DUE EAST OF COBRADIKI, PAXI SENTENCES LAMIA TO BE SET ADRIFT ON THE ICY SEAS OF MISEROS FOR ETERNITY.

THE MAGNOTAUR GIVES A LETTER TO ANATO, A SCROLL TO ALINA AND THE PIPES OF PAXI TO ALEXI, AND ORDERS HIS SERVANTS TO SAIL TO MINOS, SOUTH WEST OF COBRADIKI.

LAMIA GLARES AT THE MAGNOTAUR IN DEFIANCE. NOW SHE HAS LOST ALL HER POWERS, BUT SHE VOWS THAT SHE WILL NEVER REVEAL WHERE THE TREASURES OF MINOS LIE HIDDEN.

ALTHEA   THE SERVANTS OF THE MAGNOTAUR

This is Thebe.   This is Alexi.

Pages 68-69

Reading the document, the strange conversation that Al recorded in his diary (page 66) begins to make sense. The Cobra gang have built a machine called the COBRA (Crystal Operated Beam Reactor) and plan to use it to trigger a volcanic eruption on Magnos on Saturday. All they are waiting for is the arrival of the final COBRA consignment. At the port of Kaos (page 52), the man in the suit told Niagara and Bronson that this consignment had been held up in Enchillada. According to Al's diary, the Enchilladan consignment is a crystal. One of the COBRA's vital components happens to be a crystal of venomite. Remember the news clipping in Al's villa (page 55)? It contains an item about a stolen venomite crystal called the Serpent's Eye of Enchillada. This must be the final consignment.

Pages 70-71

The word SNAKE appears at the top of the decoded fax and along the top row of the grid on the square piece of paper, with the remaining letters of the alphabet written below. The first letter of the fax, L, has been encoded by taking the number 3 from the beginning of its row on the grid, followed by the number 4 from the top of its column. The rest of the fax has been encoded using the same principle.

As COBRA is typed at the top of Bogartus's fax, you have to draw a new grid to decode it, based on the original grid, but with COBRA written along the top row. Decoded, the fax says:

LAMIA – EYE TO ARRIVE ON DALLIANA FERRY TOMORROW MORNING AT NINE – OPHIS

Pages 72-73

According to the writing on the fresco (see pages 64-65), the island of Minos lies south west of Cobradiki and the island of Kira lies due east. Kira is on the chart, but there is no sign of Minos. If you flip back to the magazine article on page 63, you will see that Minos was the ancient name of Magnos. The only island on the chart which has Magnos to its south west and Kira to its east is Tremilos. This must be Cobradiki's modern name and this is where Nat and Lina should go.

Pages 74-75

On the stone, there are two kinds of symbols arranged in alternate rows. One is similar to the writing on the fresco (pages 64-65), while the other is similar to the writing on the scroll. Look at the third row of symbols. Could it be a translation of the second row? Thinking back to the fresco, you know what the symbols in the third row are in the modern alphabet, so you can figure out what the symbols above them must be.

Now you can decipher the contents of the scroll and locate the Throne Room. To get there Nat and Lina should enter the door in the top left-hand corner and follow the route marked in black. The rooms that they must go through are numbered in order.

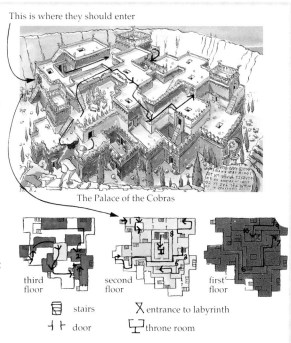

This is where they should enter

The Palace of the Cobras

third floor

second floor

first floor

▤ stairs   ✗ entrance to labyrinth

⊣⊢ door   ⊡ throne room

Pages 76-77

First, you have to figure out where the trio are. After they came to, Nat and Lina ran along a passage to a junction, turned left, then ran down a flight of steps into another passage where they met Al. At the end of this passage, they ran up more steps, then turned left and followed a winding passage around to a dead end. There is only one route they could have taken. It leads here.
On the plan of the palace (see the answer above), the symbol ✗ marks the entrance to the labyrinth. This symbol is on the plan of the labyrinth and this is where they should go. The route is shown in black.

Pages 78-79

The white scrap of paper on page 66 is the key to the sequence. You have to press five buttons to enter the secret chamber. The third button is two buttons above the first and it isn't in the top row, so it must be in the second row. The fourth button must be in the first or second row as the second button is two buttons below it. The third and the fourth buttons have the same symbol. Looking at the panel, this has to be a snake or a triangle. The fifth button is next to the fourth. If the symbol on the fourth is a triangle, then the symbol

on the fifth must be a snake. But the fifth has the same symbol as the first and the second, and the buttons which occupy the two possible positions of the first button have circles. This means that the third and the fourth buttons must have snakes and the fourth is in the top row. Now it is easy to locate the first, second and fifth buttons. The sequence is shown above.

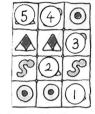

Pages 80-81

Nat can sabotage the gang's plot by turning this handle which is connected to the wheel with the laser and the wheel with the crystal. This will make it impossible for the COBRA to create the deadly V ray (see the diagram on page 69). The arrows show what will happen.

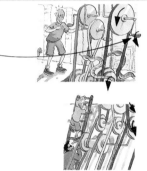

Laser   Crystal

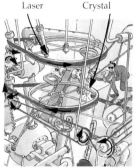

Pages 82-83

The fax is decoded using the method described in the answer for pages 70-71. Its keyword is OPHIS. It says:

LAMIA - I WILL LEAVE KAOS PORT IN M.T. AT NINE. WILL PICK YOU UP FROM BASE THEN SAIL TO MAGNOS OLD PORT TO ASSESS RESULTS OF STAGE ONE AND COLLECT COBRA GOLD.
OPHIS

This doesn't help now, but it could prove useful later on. Maybe the scroll's contents could be more helpful. The writing on the scroll is similar to that on the stone and the plan of the Cobras' palace (pages 74-75). Translated into the modern alphabet, it says:

TO THE PEOPLE OF MINOS, GREETINGS
OUR SERVANTS BRING YOU THE PIPES OF PAXI AS PROOF THAT WE HAVE CAPTURED LAMIA AND THE COBRAS. NOW YOU ARE FREE FROM THEIR EVIL THREATS BUT THEY HAVE VOWED NEVER TO REVEAL WHERE THEY HAVE HIDDEN YOUR GOLD.
TO HELP YOU FIND YOUR TREASURES, WE SEND YOU A PLAN OF THE COBRAS' PALACE, GIVEN TO US BY ITS ARCHITECT, LIRA OF KIRA. A TRAP DOOR FROM THE PALACE LEADS DOWN INTO A GREAT LABYRINTH. ACCORDING TO LIRA, ANYONE WHO LOSES THEIR WAY IN THE LABYRINTH MUST FOLLOW THE PASSAGE WITH ✕ ON ITS WALL. THIS LEADS EITHER BACK TO THE TRAPDOOR OR TO A DOOR MARKED ♋ WHICH LEADS INTO A CAVE BY THE SEA.
MAY FORTUNE SMILE UPON YOUR ISLAND ONCE MORE.
MAGNOS, NOTOS AND TOROS, PRINCES OF KIRA

(continued)

Pages 82-83 (continued)

Now it is obvious that there is a way out of the palace through the labyrinth. The route is shown in black.

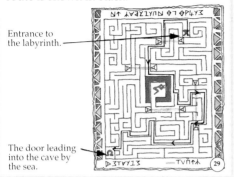

Entrance to the labyrinth.

The door leading into the cave by the sea.

Pages 84-85

The stranger is Al's boss, Strega Nimbus, alias Lamia, the Head Cobra. The telltale sign is the scar on her right arm. Now Nat knows why Strega refused to contact the police, how Al's note about the magazine message fell into the hands of the Cobra gang and who the cloaked woman at Magnos Old Port really was.

Pages 86-87

Ophis is Strega's twin sister, Amaretti Nimbus. This fits in with the contents of the fax on page 83. It was sent on September 15 – the same day that Amaretti was to be in Kaos, according to the magazine (page 63). Both Amaretti and Ophis are planning to leave Kaos at 9pm. Amaretti will set sail in her luxury yacht, Midas Touch. Could this be the "M.T." mentioned in the fax?

Along the way, you may have noticed that the fax number on the torn SFI business

fax 1 08.30 Sept 15 OPHIS 0202 08 87

card (see pages 66 and 68) matches the number on Ophis's faxes. According to the magazine, Amaretti is the boss of Sci Fi Inc (SFI).

Did you read the note to A.N. (page 69), seeking funds for the COBRA? Remember that Amaretti funds inventions. Could the note have been the starting point for the COBRA project?

Page 88

According to the fax on page 83, Ophis and Lamia were planning to collect the Cobra Gold from Magnos Old Port. Thinking back to the white scrap of paper in Al's diary (page 66), someone has removed gold from the hidden room in the Cobras' palace and taken it to the cellar of Hotel Digitalis... which is at Magnos Old Port! That must be the final resting place of the legendary Cobra Gold.

Usborne Publishing Limited proudly presents:

MYSTERY ON MAIN STREET

Written by
Tony Allan

Based on a story by
Tony Allan (What, him again?), Rachael Robinson, Mark Fowler
& Phil Roxbee Cox (That can't be his real name.)

Illustrated by
Ann Johns

Designed by
Paul Greenleaf & Ann Johns (Didn't she do the pictures?)

Puzzles by
Mark Fowler and Tim Preston

Hand lettering by
Rachel Bladon

Edited by Rachael Robinson (That kept her busy!)

Assisted by Michelle Bates

Directed by Gaby Waters

Hypnoman Comic

Written by
Phil Roxbee Cox

Designed and illustrated by
Andy Dixon (Hey, he can do two things at once.)

Lettering by
Gordon Robson

With special thanks to the mayor and citizens of Mainsville
and the makers of Disguise-O-Matic, without whose help this
story could not have been made possible.

Contents

99   Up in the Attic
104   The Crystal's Message
106   Materializing on Main Street
108   Guessing Games
110   Hair-raising Escapades
112   The Drop Before the Hop
114   Meet the Motorvators
116   Trouble on Wheels

118   Evil Intentions
120   Juke Joint Jitters
122   At the Junkyard
124   Creature Feature
126   Nightmare on Main Street
128   The Old Dark House
130   The Big Parade
132   Floating
134   Rats in a Trap
136   Saving the Stone
138   Back with a Bump

Up in the Attic

Exploring the attic in his Uncle Jack's farmhouse one rainy afternoon, Tim came across a box of comic books. They were old ones saved from when his uncle was a boy. Intrigued, Tim leafed through them and one in particular caught his eye. It was about a superhero he had never heard of before. He read on . . .

Tim groaned. The rest of the page was missing! Frantically, he searched through the box of comic books . . . and then the whole attic . . . but he couldn't find it anywhere.

He sighed and picked up the comic book again, trying to guess what happened next in the story. He was gripped. Flipping through the pages, something caught his eye. There were groups of letters dotted around the white frames of some of the pictures. It looked like a kind of coded message.

What does the comic book message say?

The Crystal's Message

Tim sat wondering about the "badge" that was referred to in the message. Just then, he heard his Aunt Polly's voice calling him down for supper. Tim tried asking about the comic books, between bites of bread, but his uncle only chuckled and said that he hadn't looked at them in years. Then Tim asked him about "Hypnoman".

The farmer looked puzzled. "I don't remember him," he said.

Tim tried to jog his uncle's memory by mentioning Troon and Droon and the evil Namtar, but Uncle Jack simply shrugged. "What else did you find up there?" he asked.

Tim mentioned an old wind-up gramophone and some family photo albums, but his mind was on the strange message he had deciphered. He couldn't wait to return to the attic.

As soon as he could, Tim hurried back up the ladder into the roof. He hauled himself through the hatch and there, right in front of him, was the missing page. Why hadn't he spotted it before?

Tim quickly scanned the pictures, and noticed something strange. The half of the Hypnostone that Hypnoman wore as a badge was covered in symbols. Tim realized it must be another message!

What do the mysterious symbols mean?

105

Materializing on Main Street

Without thinking, Tim said the decoded message out loud. The moment the words left his lips, he felt himself being jolted into the air by some invisible force.

He sensed he was being swept higher and higher. He began spinning faster and faster, and a terrible giddiness came over him . . . then everything went blank.

When he came to, he still felt dizzy. He shook his head and rubbed his eyes. He found himself by a busy street, only it didn't look like any street he'd ever been on before. The cars were bigger for starters. Then his eyes caught on something that startled him even more.

A ghostly shape was materializing in front of him. The figure looked strangely familiar. The cloak . . . the face.

"Hypnoman?" Tim said weakly, rubbing the back of his head. "But you're not real."

"Says who, kid?" the ghostly figure sighed. "The fact is, I need your help."

"*My* help?" Tim stammered. "How can *I* help *you*?"

"Right now I'm only the shadow of my superhero self," said the comic book figure, and Tim couldn't argue with that.

I can't stay materialized for long.

"There's not much I can do on my own. At least, not until I can get back into three dimensions. That's where you come in." Hypnoman continued, "I need my half of the Hypnostone to get back into action. But now it's gone, and I reckon the Namtar must have it. You've got to help me get it back. Otherwise . . ." He paused and a look of pain crossed his face. "Otherwise, the Earth could fall into the hands of this evil swine."

Tim gulped. "That still doesn't explain what I can do to help," he said.

"We've got one thing to work on – the boardgame I found in the street. The one who dropped it was the one who got me with the gas. I'd recognize him again, mask or no mask. It could be a clue. You'll find it in my hotel room. Just tell them you're Brad Bradley."

Before Hypnoman had a chance to say which hotel, he faded away to nothing. What should Tim do? This was hopeless. Suddenly a smile crossed his face. "I know where to go," he cried.

Which hotel should he go to?

Guessing Games

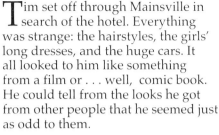

Tim set off through Mainsville in search of the hotel. Everything was strange: the hairstyles, the girls' long dresses, and the huge cars. It all looked to him like something from a film or . . . well, comic book. He could tell from the looks he got from other people that he seemed just as odd to them.

He located the hotel without much trouble and got the key to Brad Bradley's room. Searching through Hypnoman's belongings, he found the boardgame lying under some clothes at the bottom of a drawer.

Tim lifted the lid off the box. Some of the names on the board seemed strangely familiar. Then he realized that he was looking at a map of Mainsville disguised to look like a game! There were rules and a list of moves too. He guessed at once that they must contain directions, but where to?

Where do the directions lead?

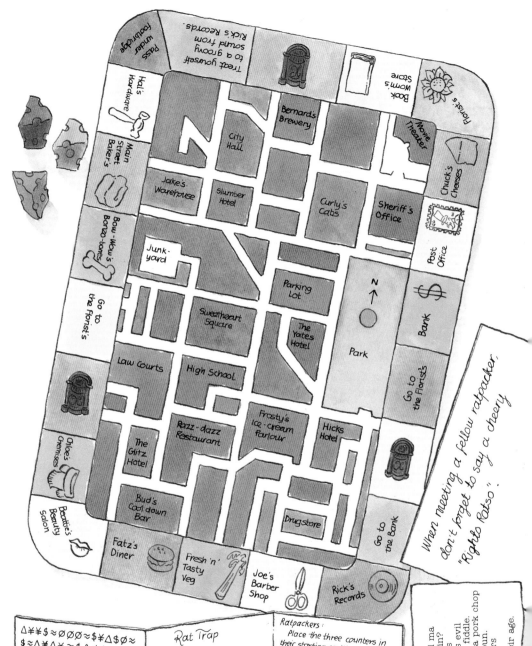

Rat Trap

RULES

TO START : EACH PLAYER CHOOSES A COUNTER AND PUTS IT ON A JUKEBOX . (NO TWO PLAYERS CAN START ON THE SAME JUKEBOX.)

THE GAME : PLAYERS MOVE AROUND THE BOARD, FOLLOWING ANY INSTRUCTIONS THEY MAY LAND ON. IF A PLAYER'S COUNTER LANDS ON A SQUARE ALREADY OCCUPIED BY ANOTHER COUNTER, HE/SHE MUST MISS A TURN.

Ratpackers :

Place the three counters in their starting positions and follow the dice throws shown below, with yellow going first :

YELLOW: 4 2 5 1 2 3
BLUE: 5 4 - 6 - 5
GREEN: 3 3 5 1 2 1

If you use the right starting position for each counter, they will all finish up on the same square after six turns. Go here for further instructions.

Food for Thought:
Remember my old ma
and her toothy grin?
Well, she still says
eating too much is evil
and plays her old fiddle.
Secretly she eats a pork chop
or a burger in a bun.
My old pa blunders
about the fort.
Great news at their age.

When meeting a fellow ratpacker, don't forget to say a cheery "Rights Ratso".

109

Hair-raising Escapades

Before setting off for the barber shop, Tim tried on one of Brad Bradley's shirts and a pair of jeans. They were a good fit. He studied himself in the mirror. He looked more like a "local" now. In his new disguise he felt better equipped to face whatever lay ahead.

Main Street was busy at that time of day. People were ordering hot dogs and playing with children in the park. Tim shuddered at the thought of the Namtar and the threat of intergalactic evil hanging over the whole town . . . the whole *universe*.

The barbershop was in the south-east corner of town. The place was packed with barbers, but nobody else. All the chairs were empty. Six pairs of eyes watched Tim expectantly. Studying their reflection, he recognized one of the men from somewhere.

Tim knew it was one of the Namtar's followers, but couldn't think where he had seen him before. Tim sat down in the man's chair and muttered "Right Ratso". He expected some kind of a reaction from him, but there was none.

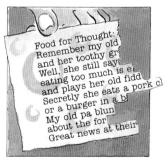

Food for Thought:
Remember my old
and her toothy gr
Well, she still say
eating too much is e
and plays her old fidd
Secretly she eats a pork c
or a burger in a b
My old pa blun
about the for
Great news at their

What he got was a haircut. Tim stared in horror at his reflection. He looked like his father did in old photos! Tim was beginning to think that he'd picked the wrong man until something was slipped into his hand.

It was a torn card, and Tim knew that he had seen one like it before. Perhaps it was a kind of message.

Which barber works for the Namtar, and can you find the hidden message?

The Drop Before the Hop

♪ BOP WOP DE LOP ♪

The note referred to the "Mainsville Hop" and, according to a poster Tim had seen, the only hop was at the high school. This was where he went next. He found the place in chaos. Everyone was helping get the hall ready for the big dance which was the school's contribution to the town centenary celebrations.

Boys were perched on ladders hanging up streamers. Girls in bobby socks were blowing up balloons.

A band was rehearsing at the front of a stage, and people were shouting. No one seemed to mind the noise because everyone was too busy getting ready to have a good time.

Tim forced his way through the crowd to the stage. He could see a trapdoor at the back that looked as if it opened onto storage space below. That was where he had to go. Quick as a flash, he lifted the trap and ducked inside.

It was dark under the stage, and there wasn't much headroom. Tim almost had to bend double. He edged along gingerly, wishing he still had the oil lamp he'd used in the attic.

He took one more step and found himself treading on thin air. He was falling, turning head over heels as he dropped. Landing with a bump, he lay still for a second, hoping nothing was broken. Then, looking around in the gloom, he found a bag. Inside was what looked like a map, and some pieces of paper. One had some sort of message scrawled on it. This had to be what he was looking for. But what did it all mean?

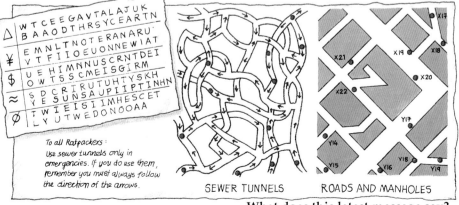

SEWER TUNNELS ROADS AND MANHOLES

What does this latest message say?

Meet the Motorvators

Tim was wondering who this "Ratman" was who had sent the coded instructions, when he heard a voice call out to him. Fighting back his fear, Tim stuck his head through the trap. Eight pairs of eyes stared down at him.

"Are you sure that's him?" asked a leather clad figure, frowning. Another one nodded and pointed. "Look, he's wearing the transmogrifier on his wrist!" Their faces broke into smiles.

It dawned on Tim that watches like his were unknown in Mainsville . . .

. . . and these people seemed to like it. A girl who seemed to be in charge slapped him on the shoulder.

"My name's Sal, and I'm leader of the Mainsville Motorvators," she said. "We've been looking for you and I'll tell you why . . ."

When we stopped off at the Main Street Milk-Bar for a shake . . .

. . . we overheard a worrying conversation.

We've fixed Hypnoman, but his sidekick - a kid with a transmogrifier on his wrist - has turned up.

Shh. Keep your voice down.

Eavesdroppers, huh?

They came to confront us . . .

. . . and we made the most of his slip-up.

"What happened next?" Tim asked.

"As he slipped, we grabbed this guy's hand," said Sal. "In the confusion, we got away with his glove, and a message he was clutching in it. The only trouble is, we can't figure out what it means."

What does the message say?

115

Trouble on Wheels

The Motorvators were impressed with Tim's decoding skills. "That's the second message I've seen from Ratman," he said, as they walked out onto the street. "He must be working for an evil outer space genius called the Namtar. Unless, of course …"

"This is no time for talking. Jump on," Sal shouted.

Step on the gas.

Eight engines roared to life. "To the junkyard!" Sal commanded. The Motorvators were ready for action. Tim hung on for dear life as the bikes shot off down the street.

"How come you got mixed up in this?" Sal called over her shoulder. Tim was about to answer when a battered green truck shot past, blaring its horn.

"Roadhogs!" Sal shouted. The bike veered as she pointed a finger at the passenger in the truck.

"Hey. I know that woman!" she yelled. "She was the one at Mainsville Milk-Bar. After her!"

Sal and Tim took off after the truck, leaving the rest of the Motorvators to head for the junkyard.

The truck rounded a corner and skidded to a halt. The woman leaped out. Before Sal and Tim could catch her, she jumped onto a passing bus moments before the door closed. Sal screeched to a halt and parked the bike.

Frantically, she waved down a cab. "Follow that bus!" Sal yelled at the startled driver. "The woman will be expecting us to keep following her on the bike," she explained to Tim. "She won't be suspicious of a cab."

"I hope you've got some money to pay for the ride," said Tim.

The cab swung around a corner just in time for them to see the woman get off the bus and scuttle down an alleyway.

Tim and Sal jumped from the cab and ran after her. Turning a corner, they found that the woman had vanished. "She can't just have disappeared," gasped Sal.

Tim pointed at a manhole cover. "She must have gone down there," he said. "Trust one of Ratman's ratpackers to use the sewer system."

"We'll never catch her now," sighed Sal, feeling defeated.

"I think I'll be able to tell you exactly where this ratpacker is heading," he beamed triumphantly.

"You don't have X-Ray eyes do you?" Sal asked. After all, Tim was a superhero's sidekick.

"No," Tim laughed. "But I do have a good memory. This ratpacker may even lead us to Ratman himself. Let's go back and fetch your bike. We may arrive before her."

Where is the ratpacker heading?

Evil Intentions

It was midday when Tim and Sal arrived at Bernard's Brewery. One of the huge wooden doors was slightly ajar. Was Ratman inside?

"After you," said Sal. "After all, it was your map that got us here." They slipped inside what turned out to be one enormous room. Empty beer barrels littered the cold stone floor.

There was no sign of the woman or any other ratpackers. Tim found a photograph of her among other items strewn across a table top. Sal's eyes widened and she pointed to the words "Sonic Boom Bomb" printed across the top of a piece of paper. "We've got to stop them," she cried.

Where has the Sonic Boom Bomb been planted?

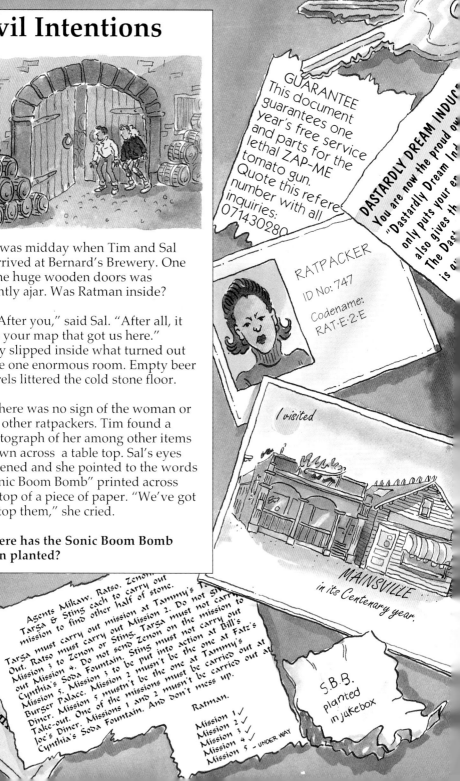

GUARANTEE
This document guarantees one year's free service and parts for the lethal ZAP-ME tomato gun. Quote this refere... number with all inquiries: 07143028O

DASTARDLY DREAM INDUC...
You are now the proud ow... "Dastardly Dream Ind... only puts your en... also gives th... The Das... is a...

RATPACKER
ID No: 747
Codename: RAT·E·2·E

I visited

MAINSVILLE
in its Centenary year.

Agents Mikaw, Ratso, Zeno... Targa & Sting each to carry out mission to find other half of stone. Targa must carry out mission at Tammy's T... Out. Ratso must carry out Mission 2. Do not si... Mission 3 to Zenon or Sting. Targa must not carry out Mission 4. Do not send Zenon on the mission to Cynthia's Soda Fountain. Sting must not carry out Mission 5. Mission 3 to be put into action at Bill's Burger Palace. Mission 2 mustn't be the one at Tammy's Diner. Mission 5 mustn't be the one at Fatz's Take-out. One of the missions must be carried out at Joe's Diner. Missions 1 and 2 mustn't be carried out at Cynthia's Soda Fountain. And don't mess up.

Ratman.

Mission 1 ✓
Mission 2 ✓
Mission 3 ✓
Mission 4 ✓
Mission 5 – UNDER WAY

S.B.B. planted in jukebox

Movie theater
ADMI...

WANTED · WANTED · WANTED

This boy is known to be working for HYPNOMAN. He answers to the name of Tim.

He is dangerous and wears this strange device on his wrist.

To: The Namtar
From: Minion, your most faithful follower.

Dear Great and Powerful One

I have discovered that here in Mainsville there are many different groups of motorbikers. These bikers are a great threat to our mission. Members of some of these gangs wear special signs on their helmets or jackets. These are the signs we know about:

The Beavers   ⊚ The Tomcats   ❋
The Wrinklies ≋ The Towts   ●
The Makaws   ◆ The Tombstones

In addition, we have gathered the following information:
Members of the Beavers ride blue bikes.
The Wrinklies' bikes do not have orange or blue stickers.
The Makaws do not ride red bikes.
The Tombstones's bikes do not have white stickers.
The Towts do not ride bikes with pink or orange stickers.
The most dangerous of these gangs is the Motorvators, but members of this gang cannot be easily identified. I hope this information is useful.

Monster: AAARRRGGGHHH!

David: If only I could distract it for long enough for Professor Jones to reach the lab.

Place
D.D.I.
Susan: Don't be a fool, David. It could crush you underfoot like some insignificant little insect.

David: It's the future of this great big beautiful world of ours we have to think about now, honey, not my own worthless skin.

Press 'activate' button

Susan: Worthless? The mistakes you made were a long time ago, darling. You're a good man. You've so much to give . . .

LEAVE!

Monster: AAARRRGGGHHH!

Susan: David! Wait . . . Come back . . .

Fellow Vermin,
Those four-eyed-do-gooders Troon and Droon have sent out an intergalactic plea for help in the guise of an Earthling's comic book.
The ratpacker who finds and destroys this pathetic plea for help shall be heaped with praises, and avoid my wrath.

Ratman

P.S Find me that other half of the stone.

MISSION 5
Planting **Sonic Boom B**
in jukebox

This bomb will give off an earsplitting scream, a nasty headaches for up to twelve hours. Once the p have fled, search for the other half of the stone.

The Sound, Fire, Power and Disarm buttons must each be wired up to one of four buttons on the jukebox. Use only one button in each row. The Sound button should be seven numbers greater than the Fire button. The Power button must be five numbers less than the Disarm button. The Fire button must not be in the top row. The Power button must not be in the left hand column.
All praise to Ratman.

119

Juke Joint Jitters

They had to get to Fatz's Diner, and fast. Sal somehow managed to squeeze even more speed out of the bike. Tim clung on as she weaved a path through the traffic. The diner lay right on the other side of town.

When they arrived, they found the parking lot thick with huge vehicles. The place was obviously popular with truckers. Sal skidded to a halt by the front door, and the two went dashing into the diner.

"We've got to get everyone out of here," said Sal pushing her way through the crowd. "The Sonic Boom Bomb could boom at any moment."

"There isn't time," Tim shouted above the noise of the jukebox. "We're going to have to try to deactivate the sonic bomb ourselves."

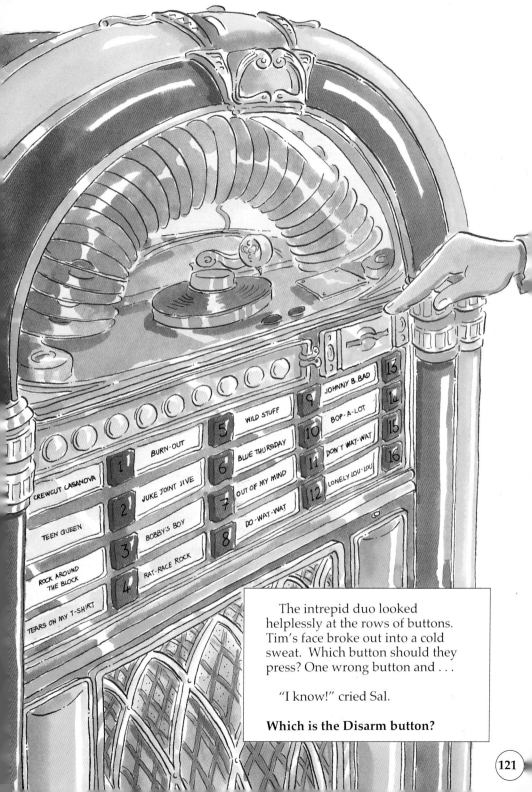

The intrepid duo looked helplessly at the rows of buttons. Tim's face broke out into a cold sweat. Which button should they press? One wrong button and . . .

"I know!" cried Sal.

Which is the Disarm button?

At the Junkyard

As Tim and Sal left the diner, Ace, a Motorvator, rode up in a cloud of dust. "Found you at last!" she gasped. "Ratman's gang caught two of us at the junkyard. We need help." They sped off to the scene of the action, swerving to avoid roadblocks that were being erected in the streets.

They picked themselves up in time to see the truck speeding out of the gates. Hypnoman faded away before their eyes, his good deed done.

"We'll never catch those ratpackers," Sal groaned.

"Yes, we will," cried Ace. "I know where they're going. And that," she said, pointing to a poster on a wall, "will help us to avoid the roadblocks."

Where are they going, and by what route?

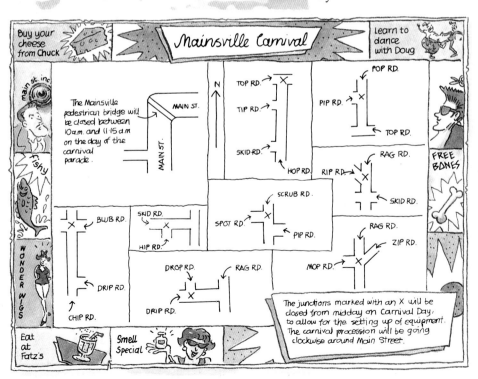

Creature Feature

Starring Nash Randall + Nanci Sparkle

Mainsville Movie Theater was full when Tim, Sal and Ace arrived. The main feature was already halfway through. It was a monster movie in 3-D, and everyone was wearing special glasses.

Tim and Sal were standing uncertainly in the aisle wondering what to do next when a voice boomed from the screen.

That sounds familiar, Tim thought. Then he remembered where he'd come across the words before. He had to do something, and fast.

What is about to happen?

125

Nightmare on Main Street

Tim scanned the seats anxiously. Suddenly a man stood up and headed for the exit. Tim was about to follow him when he noticed that the man had left something behind.

Tim ran up to his seat. A red light was winking, and wreaths of gas were starting to drift from a funnel on the top. It must be a Dastardly Dream Inducer!

Quick everyone, clear the building. You haven't got much time.

There's a Dastardly Dream Inducer in here and it's about to pump out sleeping gas.

It'll give you the worst nightmares you've ever had!

There was a stampede as frantic movie-goers fled the auditorium, tearing off their 3-D glasses as they ran. Some had already been affected by the fiendish device.

Tim and Sal pushed their way through the crowd of moaning people, trying to catch sight of the rat packer who had planted the dream inducer and fled.

"There he is," cried Ace, running up to them. She pointed to the man leaping onto a moped. "It's no good following him on my bike. It's covered in a cloud of sleeping gas."

A grateful stranger threw Tim the keys to his machine. There were six motorbikes in the pile he had pointed to, and six bike owners standing around it.

Which bike should they take?

The Old Dark House

The engine roared to life, and Sal and Ace took off with Tim hanging on for dear life behind them. "Wooah!" he moaned.

Halfway down Main Street they caught sight of the ratpacker. "Don't lose him!" Sal shouted. "He's the only lead we've got."

The moped screeched to a halt. They watched its rider pull himself over a fence.

They slunk after him, taking care not to let him know that he was being followed.

On the outskirts of town, they reached an old house. The man walked purposefully inside.

Tim made his way up to the house and peered through the window. There was no one around. Warily he pushed open the front door. The hall was empty, and he couldn't hear a sound. He beckoned to the others and they went in.

It was Tim who found the missing Motorvators bound and gagged in the basement. Mick, the taller of the two bikers, managed to hand him a piece of paper. Tim ripped off the gags.

"There was an argument between our kidnappers," said Mick, between gulps of fresh air. "One of them was refusing to take written orders from Ratman . . . until this arrived."

Tim studied the message that the kidnappers had left behind. It looked a cross between a poem and a secret code. His face broke into a grin. Suddenly, the riddle made sense to him.

What does the riddle mean?

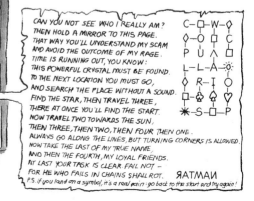

CAN YOU NOT SEE WHO I REALLY AM?
THEN HOLD A MIRROR TO THIS PAGE.
THAT WAY YOU'LL UNDERSTAND MY SCAM
AND AVOID THE OUTCOME OF MY RAGE.
TIME IS RUNNING OUT, YOU KNOW:
THIS POWERFUL CRYSTAL MUST BE FOUND.
TO THE NEXT LOCATION YOU MUST GO,
AND SEARCH THE PLACE WITHOUT A SOUND.
FIND THE STAR, THEN TRAVEL THREE,
THERE AT ONCE YOU'LL FIND THE START.
NOW TRAVEL TWO TOWARDS THE SUN,
THEN THREE, THEN TWO, THEN FOUR THEN ONE.
ALWAYS GO ALONG THE LINES, BUT TURNING CORNERS IS ALLOWED.
NOW TAKE THE LAST OF MY TRUE NAME,
AND THEN THE FOURTH, MY LOYAL FRIENDS.
AT LAST YOUR TASK IS CLEAR. FAIL NOT –
FOR HE WHO FAILS IN CHAINS SHALL ROT.   ЯATMAN
P.S. If you land on a symbol, it's a real pain: go back to the start and try again!

The Big Parade

Tim whistled. Ratman wasn't *working* for the Namtar . . . He *was* the Namtar. Tim wondered how many other names and identities this intergalactic arch- villain might have.

"Sounds to me like we're gonna need help," said Sal. "We can start by trying the Sheriff."

Back in town, the note on the Sheriff's office door said it all. Now what should they do?

Main Street was blocked solid. They gazed at the seething mass of people. "The Namtar-Ratman is probably out there somewhere," groaned Sal. "And we don't even know what he looks like."

Tim's eyes sparkled. "But if he's on a float, I think I know which one it is!"

Which float belongs to the Namtar-Ratman?

Floating

Tim pointed out the Namtar-Ratman's float to Sal. In a flash, she sprinted over to the other Motorvators lined up by the roadside watching the procession. She shouted something to them . . .

. . . then swung back into the road towards the Namtar's float, waving to Tim to follow her. The next thing he knew they were under the moving float, hanging perilously close to the road surface below.

He's tall.

Hi, Jemma. Great parade!

"Go right to the front!" Sal called, inching her way forward.

"What's the idea?" Tim cried, his eyes wide in terror. One slip, and he could be crushed under the wheels.

"When we reach the footbridge, pull that lever to disconnect the float from the driver's cab," Sal hissed.

How do they know when they've reached the footbridge?

Ooops!

32

Rats in a Trap

As the float came away from the driver's cab, Tim and Sal jumped clear before the front of the float crashed to the ground. Unaware of what was happening behind him, the driver of the float's cab carried on driving. Chaos reigned. The stranded float was hit by another which, in turn, was hit by another . . . Spectators scattered as the drivers behind stamped on their brakes, sending their vehicles skidding.

Amidst the chaos, Tim noticed a familiar, ghostly figure just visible on the sidewalk. Hypnoman looked sheepish. "Er . . . sorry," the superhero muttered. "I'm a little late to help." Then, brightening up, he added, "But I guess you guys managed fine on your own."

. . . am I too late to help?

Tim was still trying to guess what the rest of Sal's plan could be, when he caught sight of the other Motorvators. They were lined up on top of the footbridge. In their hands was something that looked familiar. Of course, the net that had held the balloons at the high school hop!

At a word of command from Sal, the net came down on the stranded float. The bikers had surprise on their side. The ratpackers were caught like rats in a trap. The more they struggled to free themselves, the more the villainous vermin became ensnared.

"Got you at last – " Tim started to shout, but the words stuck in his throat.

He had seen someone and something that made him freeze on the spot. It was obvious that their problems weren't over yet.

What two things has Tim spotted?

Saving the Stone

Tim launched himself at the Namtar, knocking the tomato gun from his hand and sending it flying. As the villain flailed helplessly in the meshes, something fell from his pocket, glinting in the sunlight. It was Hypnoman's half of the Hypnostone. Triumphantly, Tim snatched it up.

What do you kids think you're doing?

"One half to go," he muttered. "Then the universe'll be safe again." Just then a police car screeched to a halt in front of the stranded float. The Sheriff climbed out of it.

"These people are arch-villains," Tim said proudly. He handed Hypnoman the crystal.

With my half of the stone back, I feel better already.

His superhero powers restored, Hypnoman set off after the driver's cab. He returned, holding a familiar figure by the scruff of his neck.

What a day!

Here's the driver of the float, Sheriff. Another one for you to lock up.

Drats! Why don't things ever go right for me?

As the Namtar's ratpackers were led away by the Sheriff, Hypnoman pointed to the sky. Tim and Sal saw a gleaming, saucer-shaped object shoot across the blue.

The revitalized superhero pointed after the vessel. "Droon and Troon," he said proudly. "Our cosmic comrades. They must have found what they were looking for. We needn't worry about the other half of the Hypnostone any more. It's in safe hands."

Meanwhile a terrible change had come over one of the Sheriff's prisoners.

Whereabouts in Mainsville did you hide your half of the stone, Droon?

That's my secret, Troon. The main thing is that we have it back now.

Half man. Half rat. All vermin. I'll be back.

All I said was "The power is in the stone".

Rats. Here I go again!

The Sheriff stepped back in disbelief. "Would someone mind telling me just exactly what's going on?" he wailed.

Tim did his best to explain. "It all started with the message on Hypnoman's half of the Hypnostone," he said. And then he repeated the mysterious words . . .

Back with a Bump

Tim blinked. He was back in his uncle's attic. Come to think of it, had he ever really left it? He sat up, rubbing his eyes...

... and caught sight of himself in an old mirror.

Then he found a single frame from the comic book. Tim smiled.

The character standing next to the fully restored superhero looked very familiar.

Good luck, Hypnoman, wherever you are.

Clues

Pages 102-103
If you look through the comic strip you will find a hidden message. Working from back to front could be a good way to start.

Pages 104-105
Think back to the other coded message in the comic strip.

Pages 106-107
The comic strip is the starting point. Then, just keep your eyes peeled and remember that Brad likes baths.

Pages 108-109
Once you have found the right starting position for each die, you're well on your way to solving the puzzle. There are six possible combinations to try out.

Pages 110-111
Look back in the comic strip and see if you can see a familiar face. Have you seen this card before? Strangely enough, the letters which *don't* appear may turn out to be more significant than those which do.

Pages 112-113
Where have you seen these symbols before? How can you make sense of the lists of letters using these symbols?

Pages 114-115
The zigzag pattern is the key to crack the code.

Pages 116-117
Turn back to the boardgame and look for a place name. Although the scales are different, you can use the road map, sewer map and boardgame to find the essential starting point for the one-way system of sewer tunnels.

Pages 118-119
The piece of paper labelled Mission 5 and Ratman's note for his agents will help you.

Pages 120-121
Start by working out all the possible positions for the Sound, Fire, Power, and Disarm buttons. Then try out each combination to see which one works with only one button in each column and one in each row.

Pages 122-123
Start by finding the Junction of Rag Road, Skid Road and Rip Road and the others will soon fall into place.

Pages 124-125
If you flip back a few pages, the words from the 3-D movie will become even more familiar . . .

Pages 126-127
The key is to find out which bike belongs to the Towt gang. It should be easy to match the bikes to their owners from there.

Pages 128-129
The name at the bottom looks doubly familiar. The riddle is obviously an instruction as to how to find some words among the symbols. Remember if you land on a symbol, you must have gone wrong somewhere.

Pages 130-131
Read the banners and flags on the floats with care. One of the companies is somehow connected to the Namtar-Ratman. Look back to the comic strip, but don't stop there to find the answer.

Pages 132-133
A number in the picture might set you off in the right direction, but which one? You'll need some maps.

Pages 134-135
Tim has seen one of these faces before, but not in the flesh. That same person is holding a potentially lethal object . . .

Answers

Pages 102-103

This message is written from back to front and the letters are grouped in fives rather than in their actual words. If you start at the end of the last whole page and work your way from bottom to top along each of the pages the following message is revealed:

SPEAK THE WORDS ON THE BADGE TO COME TO OUR AID. IF YOU DON'T UNDERSTAND OUR LANGUAGE, THE TWENTY-SIX SYMBOLS AROUND THE PERIMETER OF THE BADGE SHOULD HELP YOU TO DECIPHER THE MESSAGE. MANY THANKS. LOOK FORWARD TO SEEING YOU. DROON AND TROON.

Pages 104-105

The symbols around the edge of the Hypnostone badge represent letters of the alphabet, starting with the symbol for the letter A after the arrow sign. The arrow is there to show the reader which direction to follow the symbols.

Using this information, decoding the message is straightforward. It reads:

THE POWER IS IN THE STONE.

Pages 106-107

Locating Brad Bradley's hotel is a matter of deduction. There are four hotels in Mainsville: The Glitz, Slumber Hotel, Hicks Hotel and Yates Hotel. They are listed on the "Welcome to Mainsville" sign in the comic strip. It is also revealed in the comic strip that Brad is staying in The Glitz as Hypnoman (look closely at the package he is left), so that rules that one out. According to a poster on page 107, Hicks Hotel only has showers but Brad is in the bath in the comic strip. This leaves either Slumber or Yates Hotel. It can't be Slumber Hotel because it is closed for repairs. A notice says so on page 106. Brad must have checked into Yates Hotel.

Pages 108-109

Each of the counters has to start on a different jukebox, so there are six possible combinations to try out. Only one combination leaves all counters on the same square at the end. This is when yellow starts on the top jukebox, blue on the left and green on the right. The square they all end on is Joe's barbershop. This is where Tim must go.

Pages 110-111

The barber who works for the Namtar is circled here. You can see him as he appears in the comic strip, as one of the Namtar's followers.

A similar card to the one on this page appears untorn on page 109. If Tim writes down the letters that are missing from the torn card and ignores the punctuation. They spell:

Mainsville hop under stage

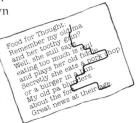

Pages 112-113

These letters and symbols only make sense when used alongside the symbols on the boardgame instructions on page 109. When a symbol appears in the boardgame message, Tim uses the first letter in the row that appears next to that symbol, then crosses it out. The next time the same symbol appears, the next letter in the row is used, and so on, until all the letters have been used.

The message reads:

> We must widen the circle. Time is running out. I must have the crystal. Ransack the junkyard, but leave it as you found it. We do not wish to arouse suspicion. My patience is wearing thin. Ratman.

Pages 114-115

Start from the top left-hand letter of the message and read diagonally down and up from left to right until you reach the top right-hand letter of the bottom row. Then carry on from the bottom right hand letter, reading diagonally up and down from right to left until you are back at the beginning again. With punctuation added, the message reads:

> I already have one half of the Hypnostone and soon I will be in possession of the other half. Once the two halves are joined ultimate power will be mine. Those loyal to me will be well rewarded. Those who fail me will suffer my vile rage. Ratman.

Pages 116-117

The ratpacker has entered Mainsville's sewer system by going down a manhole in front of a building marked "Jake's Warehouse". Jake's Warehouse is marked on the boardgame (on page 109). The manhole can then be identified on the manhole map by matching up the shape of the roads with those on the boardgame. It is manhole number X21. X21 can be found on the sewer map by its position in relation to the other manholes. From this map, Tim has realized that the ratpacker can only go to manhole Y14, using the route shown here in red. By looking back to the boardgame map you can identifiy Y14 as being by Bernard's Brewery. This is where the ratpacker must be heading.

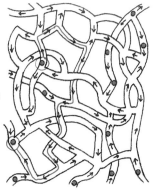

SEWER TUNNELS

Pages 118-119

By studying the three pieces of paper circled here, Sal knows that Mission 5, the planting of a Sonic Boom Bomb in a jukebox, is under way. By carefully following Ratman's instructions to his agents she can determine which mission is at which location:

Mission One: Tammy's Take Out
Mission Two: Joe's Diner
Mission Three: Bill's Burger Palace
Mission Four: Cynthia's
                Soda Fountain
Mission Five: Fatz's Diner.

So the Sonic Boom Bomb is in the jukebox at Fatz's Diner.

Pages 120-121

Sal has remembered the instructions to Mission 5 that were on a piece of paper at Bernard's Brewery. First she and Tim note down all the possible positions for the four buttons, such that the Sound button is seven numbers greater than the Fire button, the Power button five numbers less than the Disarm button, the Fire button not in the top row and the Power button not in the left-hand column. Then they look at each possible combination of buttons and find that only one satisfies the condition of there being only one button in each row and one button in each column. They find that the Fire button is number 3, the Power button number 8, the Sound button number 10 and the button which they must press to disarm the bomb is number 13.

Pages 122-123

Ace noticed that one of the kidnapped bikers had managed to write the words "Movie Theater" in dust on the side of the truck. To find the route from the junkyard to the Movie Theater, Tim, Sal and Ace must match the junctions shown on the notice board with the roads on the boardgame to find out where all the roadblocks have been set up for the carnival. First they identify the junction of Rag Rd., Zip Rd. and Mop Rd., which is between Frosty's ice-cream parlour and Razz-dazz restaurant on the boardgame. Then, using these street names, they can find out where all the other junctions are and where the roadblocks have been set up. There is only one possible route that they can take to get to the Movie Theater avoiding the roadblocks. The route is shown here in red.

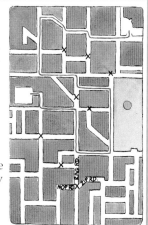

Pages 124-125

Tim hasn't heard the words from the movie before, but he has *read* them. They appear as part of a movie script in the papers they found at Bernard's Brewery on pages 118-119. Handwritten notes on the script include the letters D.D.I and the words "activate" and "leave". Another piece of paper from the brewery refers to a Dastardly Dream Inducer. Tim has realized that a ratpacker must be about to activate this fiendish device.

Pages 126-127

There are six bikes in the pile and only five of their owners standing around them (The sixth person's bike isn't in the pile). Tim and Sal must match the bikers to their bikes. To do this, they use the information Minion sent the Namtar on pages 118-119. Using this Tim and Sal work out that there is only one bike which doesn't have pink or orange stickers, so that must belong to the member of the Towt gang. This leaves only one blue bike, which must belong to the Beaver. Only one of the remaining bikes has neither orange nor blue stickers, so that must be the Wrinklie's bike. The Tombstone's bike is the only other bike without white stickers, and the Makaw's is the green one. This means that the red bike at the bottom of the pile is the only one that is ownerless and is therefore the one that they should take.

Pages 128-129

If you hold ЯATMAИ up to a mirror, you will see the word NAMTAR. The Namtar and Ratman are the same creature. The riddle also tells the followers where to search next for the missing half of the Hypnostone. Tim follows the riddle's instructions, and finds that only one sequence of letters can be made, reading LAW COU. He then takes the last and fourth letters of Ratman's true name (the Namtar) giving him the words LAW COURT. This is where the ratpackers are supposed to go next.

Pages 130-131

Tim has spotted a float with a banner marked Main Street Inc. He remembers having seen the company name before (along with a company logo of a staring eye) in an advertisement on a noticeboard on page 123. This logo was also worn by the Namtar in the comic strip. Tim realizes that this float must belong to the intergalactic arch-villain himself!

Pages 132-133

The manhole is really the key to this clue. By comparing the manhole map to the boardgame, X20 can be located in the top northwest corner of Main Street. The noticeboard on page 123 shows that the footbridge is in that corner. This board also states that the carnival is going clockwise. Tim therefore knows that he must disconnect the float from the driver's cab when he goes over the manhole.

Pages 134-135

The "someone" Tim has recognized is the man holding the tomato. He appeared in the Main Street Inc. advertisement on the noticeboard on page 123. Tim strongly suspects that this is the Namtar-Ratman disguised in human form.

The "something" Tim has spotted is the tomato itself. He recalls having seen a guarantee for a lethal ZAP-ME tomato gun in Bernard's Brewery on page 118. It's more than likely, therefore, that this is no ordinary fruit! They are all in great danger.

First published in 1995 by Usborne Publishing Ltd, Usborne House, 83-85 Saffron Hill, London EC1N 8RT, England. Copyright © 1995, 1994, 1991 Usborne Publishing Ltd.

The name Usborne and the device 🐝 are Trade Marks of Usborne Publishing Ltd.